A Twist In Time

Authored By:
E. G. Glover

To my daughter Amelia.

*As I watch you grow, I hope you see the
love my heart holds for you.*

A man's love can be his fate,

Twist his heart, his soul soon breaks.

In all things he must stand and wait,

Time can put an end to all he makes.

- E. G. Glover

Prologue

Monday, September 24, 2012

Roger could make out the rays of sunlight as it broke through the strands of Lisa's chestnut hair. He cupped her cheek with his hand, being careful as he drove down the twisting, rural road.

"Thank you for taking me to work this morning," she rasped, her voice still sounding a bit sleepy. Roger briefly met her green-eyed gaze and let out a muffled yawn. "You know I'd take you to work every morning, if I could." Lisa's lips curled into a half grin as she replied. "In just a few days, you can take me as much as you like."

Roger's imagination filled with the thoughts of their wedding-to-be, his heart overflowing in anticipation of that day. "Just a few more days. Can you believe it? Feels like we have been engaged our whole lives."

Lisa leaned across the seat in an attempt to kiss his cheek as the car pulled into the town's drug store. Roger rapidly shifted the car into park, and turned his head to meet her lips, feeling his emotions melt into her.

He reluctantly broke the kiss and gazed longingly at her beautiful curves as he placed his hand in hers. "You sure you don't need me to pick you up this evening?"

She shook her head and smiled, her hair waving at her cheeks. "My parents are going to drop off my car. It just needs new tires and my dad insisted he take it to get them changed." Roger rolled his eyes. "Your dad thinks you're so helpless." She stepped from the car, blowing him a kiss before closing the door. "I'll call you when I get home." He leaned in her direction and wagged his eyebrows at her. "I can't wait."

Roger watched as Lisa disappeared into Monroe Drugstore, noting how her white lab coat acted as though it were the cape of some serene royal personage as the door closed behind her.

Roger lightly touched his lips, already missing her kiss as he pulled out of the parking lot. He could not possibly know it would be their last.

∞

Later that evening

Roger had been scrubbing his house from top to bottom for the past week, in preparation for the day that he would bring his bride home for good. He was nearly finished with painting the bedroom.

He ran his empty hand across his forehead, circumventing the sweat headed for his eye. His other hand held a brush which was lightly speckled with cobalt-blue paint. With one final swift stroke of the brush, he triumphantly proclaimed to the empty space, "Finished! She's going to love this!"

Roger could feel more perspiration headed for his eyes and reached up to block it, realizing too late he had just smeared blue paint through in the front of his coppery-brown hair. He walked to the bathroom and gaped in the mirror at his newly colored bangs. He finally grinned, and proclaimed, "Good thing this is latex paint." Roger soaped up his hands and hair, not getting the best results with his initial scrubbing.

As he lathered up his hands again, the ringing of his landline phone could be heard over the running facet. He grumbled to himself as he turned off the water and grabbed a nearby towel from its hanger. He occasionally regretted his abhorrence of modern so-called "conveniences", such as cell phones you could mute and caller IDs that said who was calling you at such an inconvenient moment.

Roger walked to the living room, careful to dry his palms before fishing up the seemingly ancient rotary phone's receiver from its cradle.

"Grayson residence," he answered formally, trying to hide the hint of annoyance in his voice at the light blue streaks in his hair. On the other end of the phone, he could hear the sounds of a person choking back tears. "Roger, it's Gene."

The phone was silent for several moments. "I don't know how to tell you this." Roger felt his blood freeze within his veins. Roger had known Gene Franks since elementary school, and the rhythm in his voice told Roger he was delivering troubling news. Roger ran his fingers through his hair, caring nothing about the paint within it now. "What is it? What's wrong?"

"There's been an accident." More silence. "Lisa's been hurt."

The towel in Roger's hand fell to the floor, his pulse quickening with every heartbeat. "What...what do you mean, hurt? What happened?" Roger could tell that Gene was barely holding it together. "Just get to the hospital, now! I'm at the gas station, but I will meet you there."

Roger could hear the phone line disconnect as the receiver slid down his cheek. His heart's rhythm dulled within his chest as the light around him slowly grew indistinct, shattering into sharper and sharper patterns.

"Lisa's been hurt." Gene's horrified whisper repeated over and over again in his mind.

The reiterating phrase deafened him as he drove like a madman toward the hospital. He could feel the tears filling his eyes, but he refused to let them fall. He found himself hoping his lack of crying would somehow be a service to Lisa's well-being. "She's going to be okay. She's going to be okay," he recited to himself.

His hands were like vises gripping the steering wheel as he skidded into the emergency parking area. Roger didn't pause long enough to turn off his car; he hurtled toward the sliding glass doors, each step feeling like one hundred.

The fiery glow of the red emergency room sign burned into his brain as he flew through the opening, nearly falling to the ground as his foot snagged on the automatic doors. The few people sitting in the waiting area looked at him with bewildered expressions, half-dazed from their own traumas that brought them to this place.

Roger slid to a halt in front of the nurses' station, knocking a patient clipboard to the floor. The young nurse's eyes shone as bright as a new silver dollar as her mouth opened to speak. If she did, Roger didn't hear her.

"Where is Lisa Barnet?" Roger's voice shook with the fear that had consumed him. The nurse began frantically typing on her keyboard, looking through the patient list. Time seemed to slow down as he waited for her to respond. The smells of the hospital, bleach and bile, pain and panic, filled his nostrils causing his stomach to churn. To Roger, it was the all-encompassing smell of death.

As the nurse looked up from her computer screen, Gene burst from the double doors that led into the rest of the hospital. Gene's distraught and broken expression told him what he needed to know as Gene grabbed Roger with a bear's embrace. He could feel the dampness of Gene's tears against his neck. "Roger, she's gone! She's gone!"

The muscles in his legs went numb and gave way; Gene's body being the only boundary between Roger and the hard tile floor.

"What do you mean, she's gone? She's not gone! She's in there!" Gene's support gave way, and both men slid to their knees; Roger weeping uncontrollably. "Roger, she's gone. She was hit by a drunk driver on her way home." Gene buried his face in his hands, gulping back his own grief.

Roger felt the rage build within him as a whining hum coursed through his head, "Who? Who did it?" The rage within him set his blood afire. "I'll kill whoever took her away from me! I'll kill him!"

Gene grabbed him by his shirt as Roger tried to muscle by him. "The guy's dead." Gene managed to gasp through the immense effort of restraining the primal rage of his lifelong friend. "Whoever hit her, he's dead."

Roger could see his own heartbeat as each pulse distorted his vision. Gene continued, gulping between short bursts of sobbing. "He hit her head-on. His car burst into flames. The only reason Lisa wasn't burned in the crash was because she was ejected from her car."

Roger gnashed his teeth together, feeling as if they would shatter into shards. "Do they know who the son of a bitch was?" Gene took Roger's face in his shaking hands and locked eyes with his childhood friend. Gene slightly shook his head. "No, Rog. He was too far gone."

Roger's vision distorted to the point where Gene was nothing more than a washed out, featureless shape. "Oh my God," fell from Roger's lips repeatedly, each syllable quickening with the cadence of his heart.

Lisa's face, her eyes, her laugh, her beautiful smile, all flashed before Roger's eyes as everything went black.

Chapter One

Wednesday, September 18, 2013
Almost one year later

Gene stepped from his old Monte Carlo and glanced back. "You said you needed out of the house. Well? Come on." Roger sat with his arms across his muscled chest, his eyes locked onto the dash board. "This wasn't exactly what I had in mind."

Gene was worried about his friend. Since Lisa had been killed the man left his house, only to go to work. Roger had turned into a shell of the man he once was. His kindness and general happy-go-lucky demeanor had turned into a solitary black cloud. Grief this deep takes time, Gene thought, but maybe this grief is too deep to surface from. Gene watched as his friend turned to look at him, his face frozen into a frown. "If this will get you to leave me alone, fine."

Roger forced open the door and slammed it with a teeth rattling thud. He stormed off toward the door of the rustic looking wood building. Gene had known it would be a task to get Roger out of his desolate routine, but he hoped taking him to a place that fit his old interests might help.

The two men stepped onto the aged wooden porch and took in their surroundings. The forest around them was thick with the odor of pine. The sun's afternoon rays could be seen penetrating the wooded canopy. The place was deathly quiet, other than the sound of a lone crow. The bird appeared to fall from the sky landing silently on the edge of the old building's rusty gutter, not five feet from Gene.

Gene jumped at the black shape just above him, raising his hand over his head as if the bird were considering landing on him. "Damn bird! Get on! Shoo!"

Roger grinned at him and started to chuckle, surprising himself. "Looks like you made a friend." Gene lowered his arm and glared coldly in his direction. Then, he realized it had been months since he had heard his friend laugh. He smiled back at him, hopeful this plan would work. "Looks like."

The crow sidestepped back and forth on the gutter, eyeing both of the men in turn. It stopped in front of Roger and lifted a foot to scratch at its beak.

Gene studied the bird as it gazed at Roger, its dark eyes filling him with a strange sense of trepidation. Roger's face slowly resumed its previous stone state. He grabbed the door handle and gave it a push. Gene hurried in behind him, not taking his eyes off the large, winged visitor. As the door closed behind them, their attention was drawn to the man sitting behind a big hardwood desk. The man studied both friends in turn, reminding Gene of the crow outside. "Can I help you fellows?" The old gentleman took a deep draw off of an elongated pipe. Only his eyes revealed his true age, as his tawny copper face showed few lines or other signs of aging. His jet-black hair ran the length of his back and was braided, tied off with a blood red piece of cloth at the end.

Gene was the first to speak. "Um, yes, sir, I had called you yesterday. I asked if my friend and I could take a tour of the stone circle here in Salem."

The Native American took another long puff from his pipe and let the smoke circle above his head, "Oh, yes. I remember. Gene, wasn't it?" Gene smiled and offered the man his hand, "Yes, I'm Gene, Gene Franks. You must be who I spoke with yesterday?" The old man looked at his hand a moment, then finally took it and gave it a firm shake. "Pleased to meet you."

Gene pulled his hand back, hoping the old codger had not broken his fingers. The man turned to Roger, extending his hand. He grunted, "And who might you be?" Roger looked at the old gentleman in fascination, gripping his hand in turn. "I'm Roger Grayson." "Richard Adahy," the man puffed.

The imposing older man held on to Roger's hand a little longer than was comfortable, before finally releasing it. Both men stared into each other's eyes, as if in a trance.

Trying to ignore the awkwardness in the room, Gene looked around the office. A large bear skin rug and a scattering of deer heads were the only items in the room that could be called decorations. The walls were made of cedar, which put off a very calming scent.

Richard looked away from Roger and back to Gene. "You boys ever been up to Mystery Hill before?"

"No sir, never been to Salem for that matter," Gene stated, adjusting his collar. "I thought not," Richard began as he adjusted himself in his seat. "Lots of strange things up on the hill, especially with the fall equinox coming up." Roger's eyes sparkled with a hint of excitement; something Gene could not recall seeing in a long time, "What sort of strange things?"

The old man laughed as he placed the bowl of his pipe in a nearby ashtray and rose to his feet. "Come on. I'll show you."

Richard rounded the desk and passed the two men, a faint cloud of pipe smoke trailing behind him. As he pulled the door open and crossed the threshold, the massive black bird dropped from the roof and landed on his shoulder. Gene and Roger both jumped as the crow flapped its wings to gain its balance.

Richard turned back to them, a half grin on his face. "Don't mind Percy; he likes to walk with me when I go up on the hill." Roger gazed at Gene in bewilderment and followed after Richard.

∞

Walking up the old dirt path, Roger found he could not take his eyes off their black winged passenger. The bird positioned itself on Richard's shoulder so that it was staring back at him, its head slightly bobbing up and down with each step the old man took.

"So, how'd you befriend this crow?" Roger queried. "Didn't," Richard replied. "He befriended me. One day when I first bought this place, I was up here on the hill. I'd been removing some of the overgrowth off of the stones. He sat in a pine tree and watched me all day. When I finally headed home, he landed on my shoulder, just like he is now. He's been doing it ever since."

The crow twisted its head, as if understanding the old Native, and it let out an unnerving, "Cawww."

Roger could tell that Gene was terrified by the crow. As the men trekked up the hill, his face looked bleached with fear every time he caught sight of it. Roger, on the other hand, was fascinated by the appearance of the creature, locking eyes with it at every opportunity.

Gene cleared his throat before he spoke. "He doesn't bite, does he?" Richard stopped and turned. "Well, he's never bitten me," he said with a wink in Roger's direction before continuing up the trail. Their path began to flatten in front of them as they approached the top of the hill.

The crow took one more look at Roger before it bounced from Richard's shoulder and landed gently atop his head. Gene swallowed hard, hoping the bird would find something else to do. As if on cue, the crow took to the air and vanished from view.

Roger tracked the black streak as it vanished into the trees. "Where'd he go?" "He'll be back," Richard replied succinctly. Several large stones of various sizes could be seen in the distance. At first, they appeared as small specks on the horizon, but, with each step, they began to take form.

The cool September air blew Roger's hair back slightly as they entered a large clearing in the woods. He squinted at the late afternoon sun as its rays burned through an opening in the trees, somehow feeling as if it were lighting their path.

Richard led them through the rows of stones until they reached the center. Roger could make out two straight lines where the forest was void of any trees. One path lead due west; the other, due east.

Gene stood in confusion as he surveyed the area around him. "Is this it? Just a bunch of boulders in a giant ring?" Richard snapped his head toward him. "These are not merely boulders in a ring," he stated, in a tone that bordered on exasperation. "They have been here for centuries, long before Columbus ever set foot on this land. Maybe even before the Vikings landed in Newfoundland."

Gene smirked, not heeding the signs the elder found him abrasive, "Okay, so they are old, giant boulders. What do they represent?"

The commanding Native American turned so that both men could see his face. His eyes grew large with vexation at Gene's condescending comment. He quickly suppressed the irritation he felt and replied with a somber tone, "It is a calendar of sorts." He continued, lifting his arm and pointing to the west, "As you can see from the setting sun, that path marks the end of the day. If you will look very closely, outside of the circle, there is a tall stone about five hundred yards away. When the sun sets, touching that stone, it marks the fall equinox, the beginning of autumn."

Roger spoke up, "That's in a few days, isn't it?" The elder nodded, calming with the realization one of these visitors took this sacred space seriously. "On that day when the sun will set exactly in line with it." Roger had to strain to view the top of the far away stone, but it could be seen.

Richard pointed in the opposite direction, intoning, "This clearing in the trees leads to another tall stone and..." Gene butted in, "And let me guess, it marks the spring equinox?" Richard glared at him, as did Roger. Gene placed his hands behind his back, and bounced on his heels for a moment, trying not to laugh.

"Correct," Richard stated dryly. "So, that's all it does" Gene goaded, "Marks the seasons. Not all that impressive."

Roger couldn't figure out why Gene was trying to provoke the older man. He walked over and gave Gene a nudge in the side as he passed, hopefully passing along the hint for him to button his lip.

Richard placed his hands together in a meditative pose for a moment, in deep thought. "There are old legends about this place," he stated slowly with preternatural calmness, "most of which neither one of you would believe."

Gene chuckled, mumbling, "Of that, I'm sure." Despite his friend's irksome manners, Richard's words got Roger's attention. "What sort of legends?" "I really don't think your friend wants to hear it," Richard replied. Roger looked to the east stone, its top barely visible from where he stood, and could see a small black dot that seemed to move slightly. He refocused his eyes, and saw it was the crow, seated calmly. It seemed the animal was watching and listening to everything transpiring among the three humans.

Roger glared daggers at Gene again, letting him know that he had enough of his dimwitted behavior. "Don't mind him," he directed at Richard while pointing an extended index finger towards his friend. "He's just not up on anything out of the ordinary."

Gene ignored his remark and started walking around the north edge of the stone circle. Roger again turned to Richard, stating, "The old legends say that this place was once used for time travel." A stifled laugh came from Gene's general direction.

Richard seemed to take Roger's lead in ignoring Gene, and came closer, pointing again to the west. "It is said, that if a person truly believes and is standing in the center of the stone circle on the evening of the fall equinox, they can actually move into the days long past." Richard then faced the east, indicating the stone now before him. "The same is said about when the sun touches the eastern stone, except he will travel into days not yet born."

Roger's face grew pale; Richard could not tell if it was from fear or euphoria. He breathed, "And you believe this legend?" Richard nodded and whispered, "But the risk to your life would be extremely high. It is said that if it is done incorrectly, you could be trapped in an endless second of time. You would forever be locked there, with no past and no future."

At that moment, the crow flew out of the east like a black ghost, landing on Roger's shoulder. Richard smiled a toothy grin. "It seems that Percy likes you. Never before has he taken to another person so quickly." Almost without thought, Roger stretched out his arm parallel with the ground, and the crow walked the length of it. Stopping at his hand, the bird took off and headed toward the west. Roger could see him as he landed on the west stone and began to peck at it, the rhythmic sound almost like a heartbeat.

Gene walked up beside Roger, looking at his watch. He spoke in a flat tone. "It's um...time we should be getting back to Monroe."

Richard gave him a displeased look and leaned close to Roger's ear. "Come visit me without your friend and we can discuss this further." Roger nodded his understanding as the old Native American took a step forward, leading the way back down the hill. Gene, still silent, fell in line behind them. Roger could see the crow watching him as they left the circle. The bird gave one deep extended cry and flew into the woods.

Chapter Two

Thursday, September 19, 2013

Roger woke the next morning to the sound of his alarm clock screaming its usual tone. His conversation with Richard had scorched a mark of fear within him but ignited a hope where none had existed. All night he'd pondered the possibility of getting Lisa back. Could it really be possible to travel back in time and save her from the car accident? If he couldn't save her, maybe he could travel to the past and bring her to the present. Maybe he could even stay with her in her time.

His brain was on overload from all the possible options open to him. The only person that could shed any light on the subject was Richard. It was

Thursday, so Roger had the whole day to do what he wanted.

He knew his two days off from his job at the local library would typically be mind numbing. Usually, he would watch television or sleep, his best escapes from the real world outside. He jumped from his bed and dressed quickly. His mind flashed to Gene and his reaction to everything that transpired on Mystery Hill.

Roger never knew that Gene was so closed-minded when it came to unexplained phenomena. After all, it had been his idea to make the trip from Monroe to Salem in the first place. "Maybe he's afraid that time travel is possible. Or maybe he's afraid I'll try something stupid," Roger pondered to himself. He ran to the kitchen and grabbed a tonic from the refrigerator. There was no time to eat. He needed to be in Salem. He got into his car and skidded out of the driveway.

If it really was possible to get Lisa back, the risk to his life was of little consequence. He had felt dead inside since her accident, so if he actually died in the attempt, little would change.

One thing was for certain, he wasn't going to mention any of what he was planning to his friend, and he wasn't too sure how much of his plan to tell the old fellow.

∞

Hours later, Roger pulled his car up to Richard's office. He could see the crow preening himself on the roof's edge, as if he were waiting for Roger to arrive. The bird looked down on him as he exited the car; his head bobbed up and down as if he were excited to see Roger.

The crow released a call of welcome and headed for his shoulder.

At first, he started to shoo away his new friend, but decided to let him ride as he approached the office door. He pushed the door open, and the bird took flight, landing back in his original spot on the roof.

Roger found the old Native behind his desk. The older man's eyes lit up with the sight of him. "So, you have come back to hear more about the circle?" Roger wanted to start bombarding him with questions, but instead simply nodded. "Well, have a seat," Richard motioned towards the chair opposite him. He lifted his pipe from the ashtray and struck a match on his desk. He took several puffs before taking a long inhale and extinguishing the match.

Richard readjusted in his seat and leaned back a bit, finally saying, "So, what do you want to know?" Roger paused briefly and then spoke. "Everything." "Ha, everything?" Richard questioned with a bemused expression on his lined face, "I'm afraid neither of us have enough time for you to know everything."

Roger picked his words carefully, saying, "I want to know how to go back in time." Richard smiled, puffing on his pipe. "And where would you go? Last week, last month, last year, one hundred years in the past?" "I'd like to go back about thirteen months," Roger haltingly replied.

"Ha!" Richard seemed to continue Roger's questioning seriously. "That precise time? And what exactly would you do there if you could?" Roger tightened the grip on the arms of his chair, debating on telling him the truth. "There is something that I need to fix in my life, something that can't be fixed now." "Why can't it be fixed now?" Richard asked, not unkindly.

"I...lost something in the past, something that I can never get back, now or in the future," Roger spoke as he could feel his eyes burning from the emotion that was building up inside.

Richard asked in between long draws from his pipe, "And you think that by traveling backward in time you can get back what you lost?" "Yes! I am sure I can!" came the animated reply. "All it would take is me intervening to put things back the way they were."

A single tear rolled down his cheek. Roger knew that the old man noticed. Richard's face filled with concern. Leaning forward, he gently asked, "Was it something you lost, or was it someone?" Roger froze, not wanting to answer. "It was...someone. The woman that I was going to marry."

Richard blew out a long cloud of smoke and sat his pipe on his desk. "I can help you, son. But know this; I'm not the one that is allowing you to have this chance." After noting Roger's confused expression, Richard continued, "There is something about you. Don't ask me what it is. I don't understand it myself." Roger slowly shook his head, murmuring, "I don't understand."

"I have been the keeper of the secrets to this place for a long time," Richard replied, "but only one in a million can travel in the circle." "And you think that I am one that can?" "Ha, not think, I know!" the formidable Native American man cackled.

Roger absentmindedly scratched at the back of his neck, still completely lost in what Richard was saying. "How do you know? Why am I any different than anyone else that has been here?" Richard picked up his pipe and took a long, deep draw and answered, the words coming out between the puffs of smoke, "Because Percy told me."

Roger nearly fell from his seat. "Percy, the crow? You can talk to the crow?" Richard started choking with laughter and smoke, unable to hide his amusement at the lost young man any longer. "He landed on you, which means he likes you. Percy always knows who can travel in the circle, to travel to the past, or to the future."

Roger was finally beginning to think the old man was crazy, but his will to see Lisa was too strong to let himself believe that Richard was lying or mad. He pulled himself together and asked, "So, Percy has chosen others?"

Richard grinned. "Yes, he has, and before you ask about the others, it's not my place to tell. Of the dozen or so people that have used the circle, each had their own story. It's really not my right to tell the stories of others." Roger nodded slightly, understanding that Richard was keeping other people's affairs a secret.

Richard propped his arms on his desk, catching Roger's gaze. "You do realize that this is extremely dangerous?" "I don't care about the dangers," Roger fiercely whispered. "I want, no, I need my Lisa back!" "I see," came the resigned reply. "So, you are willing to risk your life to see her again?"

Roger shook his head. "Not just see her, but to be with her again, to hold her next to me. I want to see that expression of love on her face when I take her hand in mine. I miss her look of overjoyed surprise when I show up at her house unexpectedly; that flash of excitement just before I kiss her. I want it all back! I want to love her again! To save her from that bastard that killed her in the car accident! If I have to, I will stay in the past to be with her!" Roger realized he was standing unsteadily, holding to the edge of the desk for support. He returned to his seat, shakily, while Richard calmly observed him. "Well, I wouldn't recommend you staying there," Richard replied, matter-of-factly. "For a time, there would be two of you."

Roger looked at him hard, trying to understand. "What do you mean, 'two of me'?" Richard replied, as if this were a recitation of a shopping list instead of an explanation of time travel, "Well, the 'you' of the past will still be there also. That's something you will have to be very careful of. You don't want to go running into yourself while you are there."

"Why is that?" Roger felt as if the pressure inside his brain could cause it to burst without another moment's notice. Richard, though he had given this talk to others many times before, felt amusement at the naivete of this particular youth. "Ha! Could you imagine if another 'you' were to walk into this room right now? The shock alone could very easily kill you."

Roger shrugged. "Okay, so I'll stay away from myself while I'm there." Richard shook his head. "It's not so simple as that. As far as you bringing her back to our time, son, it doesn't work that way. Only you can travel, and you can't bring anyone back with you."

Roger shifted in his chair, considering the old man's words. "I understand. Then I guess my best bet is to try to stop the accident?"

"My boy, I can't tell you what to do. This is all up to you. I can only help you get to where you want to go and help you get back. I can't and won't help you make your decisions on what you do in between those times."

Roger tapped his finger on the arm of his chair, thinking of how to phrase the obvious, but probably rude in this case, question. "Okay. What do you need from me in order to do this?" Richard's look grew slightly angry and then softened, as he had lived this conversation many times before. "I don't need anything from you. I don't do this for any sort of monetary gain. I do this because you ask me to. The reasons you want to travel are motivated by your feelings, not for greed or some evil purpose."

"Fine, then let's do it," Roger hastily stated, not wanting to stop and consider any consequences of his rash decision. Richard stood up, looking down at Roger. "We can't do it until the fall equinox. Besides, I really think you should mull over your decision a bit until on a bus." Roger fidgeted at the intensity in Richard's voice. The wise one continued, "You have to make absolutely certain this is what you want." Roger rose from his seat, looking deep into Richard's eyes. "I know it is the best thing for me and for her. She loved me as much, if not more, than I loved her."

Richard's mouth formed a thin determined line. "Very well. Come and see me in three days. Get here an hour before sunset. I'll be ready when you arrive. Remember, think about this. You must not be hasty. Consider all the consequences your actions may bring, not just for you and your loved one, but all who are touched by your lives."

Roger reached for the old man's hand and gave it a grandiose shake. "Thank you! Thank you so much for this!" "Don't thank me. Thank Percy. He was the one that chose you," Richard said, pointing out the window.

Roger pulled the door open and turned toward Richard, his cheeks burning with gratitude, "I'll be back in three days." He closed the door behind him and looked up at the crow, who was still sitting on the edge of the roof. His eyes were locked on Roger like a marksman's scope. A sudden chill of fear ran down Roger's spine. Though crows didn't have lips, he could have sworn Percy was smiling at him.

Chapter Three

Friday, September 20, 2013

Gene directed his timeworn Monte Carlo down Smutty Hollow Road, the morning light reflecting in his sunglasses. He was headed towards Roger's house to check on his best friend. Gene had stopped by yesterday because of the concern that had mounted within him about Wednesday's trip to Salem. He was afraid of the impression Mystery Hill had carved into Roger's mind, and not finding him home made that worry double.

On the drive home from Salem, neither of them spoke of what the Native had said to them. Gene knew what Roger was thinking when the idea of traveling back in time was mentioned. He knew

Roger was musing over the possibility of saving Lisa's life.

Gene was convinced Richard was crazy, and feared Roger had fallen for the old man's story, hook, line, and sinker. Gene was afraid of the old man and his bird but said nothing to his friend about it.

Weeks earlier, Gene had come across an old historical magazine article about Mystery Hill, and something had told him to take Roger there. Now he wished he never had.

He slid his car in next to Roger's blue Honda Civic. Gene's pulse slowed a bit, knowing he was back at home. Gene stepped out and walked to the front door, giving it a hard knock. He could hear a small amount of fuss inside the house just before the door opened.

"Gene, come in!" Roger spat, out of breath. The spark in Roger's eyes was of a kind he had seen before. It was the same look he had seen when Roger and Lisa were together. That rekindled spark made the hair on the back of Gene's neck stand firm.

"What are you doing in here?" Gene questioned as he stepped in and closed the door. Roger motioned Gene to his usual spot on the couch. "Nothing, just going through these boxes of photos laid out on the floor in front of Roger's chair.

Scratching his head as he sat down, he finally muttered, "Why?" Roger picked up a handful of pictures and began thumbing through them, "Looking for all the photos of Lisa that I can find from last year."

Gene gave a muffled sigh as he looked down at the floor. "You're torturing yourself again, aren't you?" Roger gave no response, simply continuing to shuffle through the snapshots. "Aren't you?" Gene's voice

A Twist in Time

was clear and direct. Roger stopped his shuffling and looked into nothingness. "I'm not torturing myself; I'm remembering."

Gene picked up a small stack of pictures and began slowly thumbing through them. "I never knew you had this many photographs of you and Lisa." "We made a lot of memories during our time together," Roger replied, still gazing absently.

Gene set his pile of photos down and observed his friend, distress written all over his face. "I know the anniversary of her death is coming up in a few days but digging through all these memories is just going to make you sick. You know that."

Roger ignored him, gaping at the paper remembrances laid out on the floor. Gene shifted uncomfortably on the couch, his mind racing for the right

45

words to say. "This has to do with our trip yesterday, doesn't it?"

"What makes you think that?"

"I'm not a moron, Roger. I know that you would give anything to get Lisa back. Do you really think any of that supernatural woogie-boogie that old man spouted off to you could really be possible? I mean, come on. I know that you have a tendency to believe in some pretty odd-ball things, but surely you don't think you could time travel?"

Roger sat frozen, as if Gene's words had ripped the very life force from him. "I don't know what to believe. Yes, what Richard had to say got me thinking, but I have no idea if he was just blowing smoke up my ass or if what he said was true."

Gene's fear of the tale of Mystery Hill flashed in his mind's eye once again. "You need to stay away from that old man. If he really believes what he told us, he needs to be locked up, not listened to, especially by you. Not with the hurt you are dealing with right now. "Roger continued to stare into space, mumbling, "Maybe you're right."

Gene smiled, not only because he thought he had gotten through to his friend, but also because it lessened his fear of Roger messing with something unnatural. "You know I'm right," he laughed, a bit unnaturally.

Roger began raking up his photographs like fallen leaves and piling them on the seat of his chair. Gene bent down to help. "You do understand I'm not trying to be mean to you, right?" Gene looked up and felt he could see the anger in his friend's eyes. "I know" was Roger's only response. After scooping all the pictures from the floor, Gene gave Roger a tight hug. "It's going to be okay." "I know it is," Roger answered simply.

The tension in the air was thick as Richard's pipe smoke. Breaking the quiet, Gene said, "Well, I've got to get to the store. Give me a call this evening; we'll go catch a movie." Roger nodded his normal half-nod, "Okay."

Gene headed out the door, carrying a bit of peace with him. He hoped he had kept Roger from falling into another deep depression. Gene got into his car, backed out, and drove away.

Roger watched Gene exit the driveway as a slight grin formed on his lips. He nearly laughed at the thought of fooling his friend. He returned to his chair, lifted the pile of photos, and started sorting.

"I will be with Lisa again, and no one, not him or anyone else is going to stop me." His voice reverberated through the empty house.

Roger came to a photograph of happier times taken at the nearby drive-in theater. Studying the snapshot, he could still feel her auburn hair brushing against his cheek. The moment echoed in his head as tears coated his cheeks, "I'll see you soon, baby. I love you."

∞

Late that evening, Richard stood outside the office that doubled as his home. Percy was perched on his shoulder, scoping the landscape. The sun's rays bled through the trees as Richard slowly ran his hand over the bird's soft, midnight frame. "End to another beautiful day, isn't it Percy?" The crow cawed in reply as he enjoyed the old man's petting.

"You and I are going to be busy in a couple of days. Got to get the circle cleaned up, remove all the leaves and brush out of the clearing. Have to make sure that everything is just as it was four thousand years ago." Percy's head bobbed up and down, catching Richard's hand with each upward motion.

Richard had been living in the rustic building behind him for nearly forty years. It would be his home until the day he died. He walked the path up the hill, Percy riding with him. He'd made the trip up Mystery Hill more times than he could ever count.

Richard had been born on this land ages ago. His mother had died during his birth and his aunt raised him. When he was old enough, he was given the job of watching over the circle by his father. His father had been a strong, stern man that Richard often missed talking with and listening to his advice, which always came in the form of a story that had been handed down from one generation to the next.

Richard mind returned to the present as he and Percy reached the top of the hill. Percy flew to his usual resting place for the evening; the large, slick stone on the farthest west edge of the circle.

Richard went to the clearing's center and watched as the sun slowly set, its course just off center of Percy and his rock. He raised his hands to the sky and called to God, "Thank you for another wonderful day upon this earth. Thank you for all that you have given me in this life. I pray to be in Your sight one day, my Lord, forever and ever, amen."

At his prayer's closing, the air around him began to blow across the clearing. At first, in a westward direction, but deliberately starting to circle, as if a tornado was forming ten feet above the ground. Richard's long, dark hair blew into his face, rising and falling with each circular motion of the wind.

His hands still pointed upward; the wind slowly calmed until it was only a whisper through the trees. He lowered his arms, looked to the west, and nodded to his friend. Percy cawed in agreement with his companion's words to the heavens, and the sun disappeared behind him.

Chapter Four

Saturday, September 21, 2013

Roger sluggishly opened his eyes, trying to focus on something, anything near him. The first thing that came into his vision was the clock on the living room wall. He bolted to his feet, scattering photos in every direction.

After going to see a movie with Gene last night, he'd continued his travels down memory lane and had fallen asleep in his chair. He flew toward the bathroom and stripped off his clothes to get a shower. Being late for work was not on his to-do list.

As his pulse slowed from the boost of adrenaline, a thought crept in as he hurriedly washed his hair, "Why am I rushing?" It dawned on him there was no reason to rush, or even go to work, for that matter. Tomorrow he would be gone, and somewhere in the past. He chuckled as he washed the soap off his body, the suds forming an elongated circle at his feet.

Roger turned off the water and reached for a towel, rubbing it through his coppery-brown hair. His thoughts backtracked a bit and he realized that it would probably be in his best interest to go to the library anyway. Not because he felt any sort of duty toward his employer, but so he could sneak in a little historical research.

Once he finished drying, he tossed the towel back on its hook and made his way to his bedroom. Clothes were piled a good three feet high in the corner of his room. He smiled at the mountain of laundry; it was no concern of his anymore.

He looked through his nearly bare dresser. Eventually finding something that would be appropriate for work, he slid them on his slightly damp body and headed for the front door. He could just see the look on Miss Causey's face as he arrived for work thirty minutes late. Roger's lips curled an almost evil grin, "Like I even care what she thinks," he mumbled to himself as he got into his car and backed away from his house.

∞

Gene sat at the counter of Monroe's only convenience store. He'd bought the place a few years back, after the owner had decided to retire. He worked a few shifts a week, just to give his employees an extra day off, if they wanted one.

The store pretty much ran itself. His current workers were some of the best he'd had since he took the place over. They were always on time, and rarely called out of work. That made his job as owner a little too easy. Just paperwork and paying the bills.

He rested his arms on the white speckled counter, daydreaming about the movie he saw with Roger last night. It wasn't the best film he'd ever seen. The plot was cliché, the special effects were not so special, and the ending left him with a muddled look on his face. Regardless, it was nice to spend some time with his friend before having to work the next day.

Saturdays were generally slow until the evening. Their sleepy town really didn't move much on the weekends, other than the teenage crowd that would come in and take advantage of the two pool tables or three arcade machines in the back of the store. Gene had often thought of taking them out because they brought in little money. He made his decision to keep them for the simple fact that it gave some of the teens a place to hang out and stay out of trouble.

Another reason that weighed heavily in his choice was that he had played pool there as a kid. No need to be getting rid of a simple town's staples. While his thoughts continued to drift, a car pulled up to one of the islands outside. The purple Mustang was hard to miss as there was only one around the area. Gene rose from his seat and looked out the window, waiting for the car's owner to step out.

He felt his heart pick up a bit at the sight of the red-haired beauty that emerged. Gene had a thing for Heather ever since she had moved to Monroe two years ago. She'd divorced her husband and moved to the quiet town to get away from the hectic city life of Manchester.

Gene calculated the best thing to say to her as she walked toward the door, her dress of creams and browns hugging on her hips. The door opened and he greeted her with a sheepish grin, not wanting to look too eager to speak to her.

"Hey, Gene," she greeted, her eyes as green as the finest emeralds. "Hey, Heather. How are you on this fine Saturday?" Not the best line he could think of, but it would do. She tossed her hair over her shoulder before replying, "Ugh, gotta take my pony to the repair shop again. The brakes are starting to scrub."

"Has it been doing it long? "Gene asked with genuine interest. "No, just started yesterday. I want to get it fixed now, so I don't have to get a new set of rotors to go along with the brakes." Gene was impressed. Most girls he knew didn't know a brake rotor from a steering wheel.

His heart burned with wanting to ask her out, but his brain and his mouth were not working in their usual fashion. "I need to get twenty on the pump," she said as she slid a bill across the counter. He took the twenty and rang up her purchase. "Anything else I can get you today?"

Heather grinned at him and replied, "That's it for now. I'll see you the next time the pony needs some juice." She turned and headed back to her car; Gene's eyes glued to her bottom. After she was out of earshot, he started cursing at himself under his breath, "Idiot. Why didn't you ask her out? Stop being such a chicken shit."

He started to go out after her, to inquire if she would like to go out on a date. Then his common sense kicked in. He realized how desperate that would look, him asking her while she stood there with a gas nozzle in her hand.

Gene watched out of the corner of his eye as she finished pumping her gas, got into her car, and drove away. He plopped his head down on the counter, beating himself up inside for not asking her on a date. He sighed as the Mustang disappeared from sight, "One day, Gene, you're going to have to grow some balls."

∞

Monroe's library was in a small, brick and metal building near the Police Station and City Hall. The little Honda Civic rocketed past both, Roger not caring if he got a ticket or not. Luckily, the city's two policemen were nowhere near the station house as he swerved into the nearest parking spot on the street in front of the library. He had an agenda while he was at work, and it wasn't to check out people's books for them.

While speeding his way there, it occurred to him that the library had several books on historical locations in

New Hampshire. There had to be something about Mystery Hill located in them, or perhaps in the library's archives.

Roger jumped from his car and pushed the door closed behind him. He was ready for a tongue lashing when he walked in. Miss Causey was stickler for punctuality. He had thought about coming up with a lie, but what was the point? He wasn't going to be around much longer anyway.

Adjusting his clothes one last time, he opened the library door and walked in as if nothing was odd with being thirty minutes late.

Miss Causey sat behind the checkout counter, her eyes flicking from Roger to her watch and back to Roger again. He walked behind the counter, pretending not to notice her rudeness. He walked to a stack of books and began scanning them in. The vibes off his coworker were blistering.

"Well?" she erupted. He picked up another book and ran it under the laser, a beep signaling the book's return to stock. "I over slept," he said, deadpan. "That's the fifth time this month you have been late," her eyes burned holes in the back of his head as she stared at him through her large, rimmed glasses.

Roger took a deep breath before speaking. "I'm not going to stand here and make excuses. I had trouble sleeping and didn't wake up on time. End of story. If you want to make more out of it, please, be my guest." Miss Causey wouldn't have been more surprised if he had slapped her across the face.

She picked up the book she had been reading and quietly turned the page. A grin of contentment formed on Roger's face. He turned in her direction, studying her aging features and graying hair, "There's another thing. I won't be able to come in tomorrow. I...have to leave town for a while and don't know when I will be back." She spoke without looking at him, "Then I suggest you call Susan to get her to cover your shift." "Fine," and he turned back to his stack of books.

He had no intention of calling anyone. If Miss Causey fired him for it, it made little difference to him. Roger finished scanning in the returned books and placed them on a cart to take them back to the racks.

He rolled the cart over to the historical section and parked it to the side. His eyes went up and down the shelves, his mind trying to match his query. He soon found a book titled *Legends and Myths of the New England Area*. He snatched it from the shelf and placed it on his cart.

As he went up and down the aisles placing books in their proper places, Roger opened the book and laid it across the top of the cart where he could see it. Within a few minutes he found a section dealing with New Hampshire. He stopped walking so he could examine it more closely, and flipped a few pages before seeing the bold words:

Mystery Hill - America's Stonehenge

America's Stonehenge is an archaeological site consisting of a number of large rocks and stone structures scattered around roughly thirty acres within the town of Salem, New Hampshire. It is estimated to be somewhere on the border of four thousand years old.

At its center is a large circle of stones with two ten-foot-tall vertical stones on the east and west edges that mark the spring and autumn equinoxes.

A number of hypotheses exist as to the origin and purpose of the structure. One legend suggests that it is a kind of portal, allowing persons to travel to different places in time. However, little is known on how someone could use the circle in order to make such a journey.

It has been said that some people who visited the site experienced moments of 'missing time'. For example, an individual from New York state claimed she hiked up the hill to explore the stone structure, an endeavor that should have taken no more than two hours. Upon returning to her car, however, she discovered that almost six hours had passed.

Of course, there is no proof...

"Roger!" He jumped at the sound of Miss Causey's voice. Snapping the book shut, he turned to her, "What?" was all he could muster in response.

"I want you to go home. You aren't doing anything other than wasting time. I've called Susan and she said she would be here in an hour." With that, Roger slammed the book onto the cart, and marched toward the door, not uttering another word.

∞

Richard busied himself at the top of Mystery Hill, his black feathered friend watching him with a wicked delight. He had managed to remove all of the random twigs and small tree branches from within the stone circle. A sweeper made of broomcorn sat propped just behind him. Taking the handmade broom, he started at the east side of the circle and worked his way toward the center. Walking to the west side, he repeated his action leaving a two-foot-high pile of leaves and brush at the circle's north edge.

Setting his sweeper aside, he pulled a red paisley handkerchief from his pants pocket and wiped his forehead. He smiled over his work and looked to Percy, who was sitting on the far eastern stone, "I think that should do it. Now all I have to do is burn this pile of leaves and I think we will be ready for tomorrow evening."

The crow gave a loud caw and coasted over to Richard's shoulder, as if acknowledging the hard work. He twisted his head to get a good look at Percy, "You ready to set this baby ablaze?" Percy answered with the bobbing of his head.

Richard reached into his back pocket and removed a box of matches. He collected his broom, took a few steps away from the mound of leaves, and removed one of the red and white tipped sticks from the box.

Percy lowered his head toward the human's hand as he struck the match on the heel of his boot. He held the flame away from his body and Percy took the burning stick from him. Like a black streak of lightning, the crow cruised over the leaves and dropped the match almost dead center.

Percy returned to his perch on Richard's arm as the brush began to catch fire. He walked to a nearby stone as he struck another match, placing the flame into an old lantern that had been permanently attached to the large rock.

He turned back to blaze behind him and watched as the fire mirrored in the crow's eye, like the reflection on the surface of a black sea. As he stared into the fire, he felt mesmerized by the flames as they licked the air.

The sight took him back to a time he had long forgotten, when the tribe of his father had covered the land. A time when he'd been young and scared of the path that lay before him.

∞

Richard's father approached him one evening while he sat near the fire and called his Abenaki name, "Awansen. Tomorrow it will be time for you to go on your long journey, the one you have been preparing for this past season."

The fire light flicked in Awansen's eyes. The fear of what tomorrow had in store for him made every hair on his body stiffen, as if a hurricane of chilled air had twisted around his backbone. He had known when the turning of the season had come, it would be his duty to God, or Tabaldak in his native tongue, to stand amid the stones and let the air take him away.

His father placed his hand on his son's shoulder, "I know you are afraid. Two of your elder brothers have been lost in the great void, but they were not as strong as you, Awansen." The Chief removed his hand and gave him a quick rub on the back, "Even your name is derived from the journey for which you are about to take, traveling in the air by the stones."

Awansen had been told his whole life that his name meant 'air' and 'stone' in the Abenaki Language. It was never clear to him why, until his father had come to him and explained the task that was required of the Chief's son.

His father sat next to him, took a stick, and poked at the fire with one end. "You will become the guardian of our people's greatest gift from Tabaldak." Awansen frowned in thought, then spoke, "Father, once I make the journey, how will I know what actions to take once I am there?" The chief smiled at his son, saying, "Tabaldak will send you one of his flying messengers, and he will always be at your side."

Awansen took comfort knowing he would not be alone in a strange land. If he survived the journey, he would forever leave his tribe. He would never see his father again. As the fires burned to cinders, Awansen looked to the sky and prayed to Tabaldak that he would survive what was required of him. It was for his tribe and for his God.

∞

Richard snapped out of his vision and looked at the stones around him and then turned his head upward to the heavens. This land was his home, but this time was not his. His birth had been nearly four thousand years ago, when the terrain was still pure. As the fire grew taller, he could almost see himself in the flames. Not as he was today, but as a young man in his twentieth year.

Richard looked at the crow on his shoulder and recalled his father's promise of God's flying messenger that would never leave his side. He smiled at Percy and stroked his dark feathers. "My father was right."

Chapter Five

Sunday, September 22, 2013
Autumn Equinox...

Roger bustled about his house, trying to think of anything he would need to take with him to Salem. The day before he had stopped by the bank and removed what little bit of cash he'd accumulated over the years. He had no clue how long his visit into the past would be, but it was a journey he didn't want to take without some money on him. He might be there for a long time.

Roger dug deep into his bedroom closet and removed an old army duffel bag. He shoveled in as many clothes as it would hold and hoped it would be enough. Zipping the bag closed, he tossed it over his shoulder and walked into the living room.

Pictures of Lisa were still scattered on the floor. He bent down with a groan from the load on his back and retrieved his favorite photo of her, his hair falling into his face. Roger's eyes took in the image on the rectangular shaped paper and his heart grew heavy once again. "I'll see you soon," he whispered, his lips barely moving.

As he approached the door to leave, he realized that his best friend would no doubt be around to check on him at some point. He sat his heavy bag next to the door and found a sheet of paper and a pen.

His mind dug deep, searching for what to say to his friend. "Might as well just tell him like it is. Who cares if he thinks I'm crazy?" he mumbled as he pressed the pen to the white sheet. Within minutes he was finished and opened the door, sticking the note in the edge of the small window in its center.

Roger picked up his load of clothes and shut the door behind him. It was a two-and-a-half-hour trip from Monroe to Salem, and he didn't want to be late. But first, he had to pay someone a visit in Barnet, Vermont.

∞

The gray clouds above dropped a wet mist on Gene's car as it came to a stop in Roger's empty driveway. A scowl formed on his face as he noted Roger's car was missing. He shoved the car into park, not taking time to cut off the engine, and made a beeline to the front door.

His mind raced, considering where his troubled friend might be as he lifted his hand to take the doorknob. A folded piece of paper caught his eye. "A note?" Gene thought to himself as he plucked it from the door's window. His heart filled with dread at what he might find scratched on the loose sheet.

Unfolding it, Gene leaned his back against the door, not wanting to believe the words on the page.

Gene,

I'm headed to Mystery Hill to be with Lisa again. You can call me crazy if you want, and maybe I am, but if Richard can get me back to her, I have to try.

I ask that you don't tell anyone what I intend to do, especially my family. They would never understand. I don't know that I understand it myself, but if there is some way for me to travel to the past to be with my Lisa again, I'm willing to risk my life to do it.

I know that you don't believe that time travel is possible, just know that I have to do this. If you were in my shoes, I think you would do the same.

I'm going to visit Lisa's grave one last time before I leave town. Goodbye my friend.

Roger

Gene bolted to his car, the note still in his hand. The old Monte Carlo's tires squealed relentlessly as it swerved into the road. He jerked the car into drive and bottomed the accelerator, leaving a quarter inch of tread on the pavement. "Damn fool!" He cursed at the air.

The cemetery was only a few miles away. Gene prayed he wasn't too late.

∞

The rain had finally ceased when Roger arrived at his destination, leaving the air heavy and thick. Nearly as heavy as his heart, though he honestly wondered how that beating muscle within his chest had survived the last year. He walked the familiar path through Barnet Cemetery, staring at the ground below his feet. His brown leather shoes were marred from lack of care. He could make out the small trail he had worked into the ground over the past weeks and months.

Roger pushed his coppery-brown hair out of his blue eyes as he watched a car speed into the cemetery's circular driveway. He stared back at his feet, nearing his destination. "Damn him," he mumbled under his breath as the car slid to a stop behind him.

The cool breeze that buffeted him made him shove his hands into the pockets of his black jacket, as he tried to ignore the sound of the slamming car door. "Roger!" He heard from yards away. The sound of foot falls grew closer.

He stopped at the foot of a grave and fell to his knees, tears flooding his eyes as they always did when he looked at the name on the marble stone's face.

Gene stopped behind him, his breathing labored as he spoke, "Roger, is it true? What you wrote in that note?" He placed his face in his hands, ignoring his friend. This was his place of refuge from everyone he knew. It was his, where he came to be with the one person that he loved more than life itself. In his mind, Gene was an intruder. Roger had hoped his friend would have found his note much later.

Gene placed his hand on Roger's shoulder. He jumped at his touch but didn't remove his hands from his face as he continued to weep. "You're crazy! You know this isn't going to work. I don't care what that witch doctor lunatic told you, it's not going to bring Lisa back!"

Roger blinked once, just enough to clear his vision, and read the writing carved in the marble headstone.

Lisa Barnet
Born November 19, 1978
Died September 24, 2012
Beloved daughter
In the arms of our Lord

Reading the words surged another wave of sorrow through his body, a wave as thick as the ground that kept him from holding his Lisa.

Roger croaked as he tried to speak, his voice subdued and lifeless. "I don't give a damn what you believe. I can't bring her back from the dead. This is the only way." Gene replied softly, and not unkindly, "And what if it doesn't work? What if it ends up killing you?"

Roger bolted to his feet, knocking Gene's hand away. "I'm already dead!" he cried. "Don't you get it? I can't live without her! Our wedding was just five days away! Five days, and that bastard drunk driver took my Lisa away from me!"

He crumpled to his knees again, his outburst using up his remaining energy. He slowly crawled on all fours next to his beloved Lisa. He lay on his belly, his face buried in the grass as the tears poured from his eyes like a spring.

Gene stepped closer to him as he spoke, "Do what you have to do. I have watched you fall apart over and over again, Roger. You won't get help. You won't talk to anyone about this. It's like you died with her." Gene scratched at his short blonde hair, and he turned to leave. "I will keep your secret, like you asked me in the note. Like anyone would believe me anyway. You and I have been friends a long time, but may God help you and even your family if you are wrong."

Roger could hear Gene walk away and get into his car. He was hit with one painful outpouring after another, as the memory of Lisa swept through his brain. His insides felt as though they had liquefied from all the anguish locked within him. Roger balled up his fists into the soft grass beneath his hands, "So what if I die?" he mumbled to the ground.

∞

Gene pulled his car door closed and rested his head on the steering wheel. He turned his head slightly to see his friend lying in the middle of the cemetery, hugging the ground that had long ago accepted the remains of his beloved. Gene reached over to the passenger seat and picked up the note with his name written across the top. He scanned it one more time as he put the car in gear to leave.

The same two words jumped out at him as he read it once more. Time travel. "I hope you're right, Roger. For your sake, I hope you are right."

Chapter Six

Water coated the sides of Roger's blue Honda as it sped southeast. He knew he had to arrive at Mystery Hill before sunset, or it would be at least another year before he could attempt what he was about to do. As the road curved in front of him, all he could think of was seeing Lisa again. Beads of sweat rolled from Roger's forehead, his anticipation mounting with every mile he traveled.

A shroud of fear blanketed his body as he tried to grab hold of the last bit of hope planted deep in his mind. "Richard couldn't lie to me about something as important as this? I will believe! I have to believe! I have...," the sound of his own voice reverberated in his head.

Roger looked at the clock on the dashboard and shifted his eyes to the right to be certain the large duffel bag he had brought was still in the seat. He checked the car's mirrors and took a quick assessment of his surroundings. He felt as though the world was closing in on him. The trees outside looked strangely low to the ground as they whizzed by at sixty miles an hour.

A slight ringing filled his ears, mixed with the cadence of his own heartbeat. He slid his hand across his forehead, removing some of the perspiration that had collected just above his eyes. Roger took several deep, exaggerated breaths trying to slow his pulse. "Is this what it feels like to go insane?" His words left his mouth with a whisper, but they rumbled in his ears like thunder.

A large group of birds flew from a stand of trees nearby, crossing Roger's path. His mind immediately went to the crow at Mystery Hill. Roger remembered how the bird looked at him, his eyes full of intelligence.

The thought of the bird, his black feathers shining in the sun's light, brought the peace that he needed. "Percy," his mouth forming a smile over the name as it slipped from his lips. The animal seemed to answer him in his mind, "Take care. You should see her again soon. All is not lost. A wrong from your past can be put right. The power lies within you. Only you have the control to make things as you wish them."

A single tear rolled down Roger's cheek. His pulse slowed and his mind opened wide to the words that echoed in his brain. Roger's vise-like grip on the steering wheel diminished, and his focus went back to the road in front of him.

Percy confirmed the legend was real, and Roger took pleasure in that simple fact.

∞

Gene had left Barnet Cemetery with a deep feeling of regret in his heart. He felt it was his fault that Roger was going on this crazed wild goose chase. Of course, Richard could no more send Roger to the past than he could grow wings. Would agreeing with Roger's delusion make his friend's mental state even worse? What condition would he be in after waiting in vain in the center of that stone circle with that crazed old man feeding his fantasies of rescuing Lisa?

Gene drummed his fingers on the edge of his car's faded door handle as he drove toward the nearest gas station. He'd argued with himself the entire trip home about what to do, and he knew he couldn't abandon his friend. He pulled his car into a seedy looking truck stop and squeezed in between two large tractor trailers with just enough space to get near a pump.

Credit card in hand, he grabbed the dirt smeared pump handle with one hand and slid his card with a quick jerk of his other wrist. Sliding the nozzle into the tank, he locked the handle and stared at the gray sky. A flock of black birds flew from the truck stop's dented canopy, circling twice before finding a formation and headed east.

Gene's thoughts went to the crow at Mystery Hill, and he could almost see its coal black eyes studying him. A voice, as if on the wind, whispered in his ears, "Do not interfere with what your friend has to do. What is done is done. You cannot change it. Only he has that power."

Gene started with a nervous jolt as the gas pump handle clicked off, signaling the car was full. He shook the voice from his mind and tossed the handle back into its cradle. Jumping into his old Monte Carlo, he twisted the key and jabbed the car in gear.

"All this is just my imagination," he lied out loud. He could still hear a faint whisper in the back of his mind, and a shiver went through his entire body. "This is bullshit, and I'm going to put a stop to it now!" He yelled, hoping to convince himself he hadn't heard the voice in his head. Gene turned up the radio trying to quiet his mind as he made his way to Mystery Hill.

∞

The western wind ruffled Richard's long, dark hair while he knelt in the center of the stone circle, praying. Hands clasped near his forehead; his lips moved slightly as his inaudible words reached into the heavens. He gradually opened his eyes to witness Percy fly past his line of vision.

The bird landed like a fallen leaf on the largest stone at the far west side of the stone ring. Sunlight broke through the pass in the trees just behind Percy, making Richard squint his eyes. He rose from his knees, shielding the blinding light from his vision. Percy ruffled his feathers and cried out to him.

Richard nodded a response and spoke, "The sun sets in the west to close the day and take one traveler to a time past." The bird cried out again and flapped his wings as if to call the sun down to the horizon.

Richard looked at his watch and realized it was not long before sunset. He hoped Roger wasn't late. His ears perked to the sound of a car pulling up at the base of the hill. "That must be our traveler now," Richard stated with a slight grin.

He knew this young man was deeply filled with grief and his intentions were to save the life of the woman that still dwelled within his heart. It was a selfish wish, but a noble one.

Roger bound up the side of the hill with a duffel bag over his shoulder as he came into Richard's view. The Native waved him in his direction as Percy carefully watched him approach.

Roger was winded from his spirited climb. "I see you made it," Richard called as way of greeting. Roger took a long inhale, taking in enough air to answer his question, "I was...afraid I was going to be late." Richard shook his head, "No, you are right on time. Come. Stand in the center of the circle. We have to get you prepared for your journey."

Walking up to Richard, Roger sat his bag at his feet. "Prepared?"

"Yes," Richard intoned in a serious manner. "We must get you mentally prepared for your transition from this time to the one you are about to enter." Roger looked at him bewildered but nodded.

"First, kneel here," Richard pointed to the center of the circle. Roger complied without hesitation, his duffel bag at his side. "Now, "he asked, "exactly when do you want to arrive in the past?"

"Lisa was killed on the evening of September twenty-fourth of last year." Roger shuddered to state this date so matter of factly, as if it were not the worst day of his existence. Richard thought for a moment, "That was on a Monday, correct?" Roger started, more than slightly impressed with the old fellow's ability to recall minute details such as this. "Yes, I believe so."

"I can send you to the evening of the autumn equinox. Saturday, September the twenty-second. That will have you arriving just two days before her death." Roger pondered this. "So, you can only send me to dates of the autumn equinox?" Richard nodded, replying, "Correct. I could send you to an earlier equinox, a full two years back, but I would not advise it."

"Why?" Roger asked, thinking the more time to avoid the tragedy, the better. Richard shook his head. "The farther you travel back in time, the more likely you could get lost in the void." As Roger looked up at his guide, a twinge of fear crept up his spine from the dread in the other man's voice. "The void?"

"The void, the vortex which separates one point in time from another. If that happens, you will be left floating in an endless moment of time, never dying, existing in the heart of nothingness forever. That is why it is vital that you listen to me and follow my instructions."

Roger swallowed hard and nodded his understanding, "How will I get back after I save Lisa?" Richard tried to smile reassuringly. "Don't worry about that now. I will be there to help you return to the present." Roger brightened, hopefully asking, "You are coming with me?" Richard shook his head. "No, but I will be there."

The look on Roger's face proved he didn't understand what he meant. "Don't worry about that now. Your concern is with getting there first." Richard could see sweat forming on the young man's forehead as he paced around him, and continued, "son, you have nothing to fear if you do exactly as I say. Just listen to what I tell you." "Okay," came the returned whisper.

Richard stopped in front of him and looked down into his worried face, "I need you to close your eyes, and concentrate on my voice." Roger did as he was instructed. Richard placed his hands on Roger's head. "Now, I need you to completely clear your mind. Think of nothing but the date of September the twenty-second, two thousand twelve. Keep your eyes closed and concentrate."

∞

With Richard's hands resting on his head, Roger tried to totally empty his thoughts. It wasn't an easy feat. His lids closed tightly as he concentrated on the date he wished to travel to.

"September the twenty-second, two thousand twelve," Roger said it over and over in his mind.

He could feel the breeze around him start to pick up, blowing his hair to the right slightly. Roger licked at his lips, the cool air drying them as he quietly mumbled the date. He could hear Richard start to chant in an unknown language, his voice barely audible over the increasing winds.

Richard's hands left his head; Roger could hear footfalls as he stepped away from the center of the circle. The air around him amplified in motion, making it nearly impossible to hear the ancient tongue being spoken to him.

He heard Percy call out in what sounded like excitement, not fear, as the wind began to twist in a counterclockwise motion around him. He wanted to open his eyes, to see what was happening, but he feared the consequences if he broke his concentration. "September the twenty-second, two thousand twelve," he started yelling over the swirling gusts circling his body.

Roger heard the same calming voice echo in his ears that had filled his mind earlier in the day, "Don't be afraid. Concentrate on the date you wish to travel to, and you will be safe." "Percy?" Roger cried over the winds.

As the air around him roared like a thunderous beast, he felt the ground underneath him begin to soften, like kneeling in a mound of sand. Within seconds he became weightless, drifting like a lone feather, his body free-floating with nothing above or below him.

He had to look; he had to see where he was. Roger cracked an eyelid the width of a hair and a blinding blast of light came pouring into the sliver. His hands cupped over both his eyes, trying to block out the pain.

"Think of the date!" The voice boomed again. Roger resumed chanting the month, day, and year, over and over again, his body isolated and disjointed from everything.

Was he floating or falling?

He couldn't tell.

Had he made a mistake? Was he trapped in this whirlpool of nothingness?

"The date, think of the date!" He screamed to himself.

His chanting was cut short when his body crashed onto a hard lump, knocking the air from his lungs. Roger wheezed in pain; his arms out wide as he tried to gather his whereabouts. After several long drags of air, he was able to maneuver his body into a sitting position.

He feared to open his eyes, afraid the fierce pain would return. The air around him was still. There was almost no sound at all. "Am I dead?" He spoke aloud, not meaning to do so.

A familiar bird's cry burst into his ears, followed by another voice, "Ha! Far from it, son!"

Chapter Seven

Richard stood at the far north end of the stone circle and passed his hand through his hair, the wind slowing to a mere whisper. The air still twisted at the center of the circle, forming a small cyclone of dirt that slowly dissipated into nothing. Percy rested on Richard's shoulder, staring at the spot where Roger once knelt.

"Cawww!" Richard gave him a reassuring pat on the head as the sun faded away on the horizon. A pair of lights could be seen approaching the bottom of Mystery Hill. He frowned at his feathered friend, "Uh oh. This looks like trouble coming."

Percy took flight and glided down the steep hill. Richard took to the path that led to his office and the source of the lights. He found Gene pounding his fist on the locked office door. Percy flew over Gene, narrowly missing his head.

The young man shrieked in horror as he ran back to his car to avoid the bird's outstretched talons. He slammed the door shut within seconds of Percy landing on his hood with a sizable thump.

Richard approached the car and looked at the frightened Gene who was staring at him through a partially rolled down window. "Son, the door's locked. I was up on the hill."

"Where's Roger?" His eyes filled with horror, never breaking their gaze from the crow's presence on his hood. The bird's nails screeched against the car's metal, sending tremors throughout Gene's body. Richard kindly smiled at Gene and placed his hands on his hips, saying, "He's gone from here. But don't you worry; he made his trip safely."

"Trip?" Gene yelped, momentarily breaking his focus on the massive black bird. "You really don't expect me to believe you sent him to the past, do you?" Richard walked closer to the car, still smiling. "I don't expect anything from you. But I hope you don't expect to find your friend here, well, at least not right now."

Gene shook his head, Richard's words causing the look of terror on his face to vanish in a flash of rage. "You are a crazy old bastard!" Percy cawed at the windshield, as if warning Gene to watch his words. Richard's laughter filled the air as he looked at the young fellow hiding behind the glass. "If all goes well, your friend will return in March." Gene swallowed hard, then shouted, "March, you mean six months from now? You really are crazy!"

Richard's face dropped the smile and became stone-like, the seriousness filling his old eyes. "Son, you know that I'm not crazy. Percy spoke to you and warned you not to interfere. Go home. This was your friend's wish. If he is successful in his endeavors, you will know."

The young man's head fell to rest on the car's faded steering wheel, announcing to Richard that Gene knew he spoke the truth. He raised his head, "And if he's not back in six months?" The crow came to rest on the car's windshield wipers, eyeing him with a devilish glower. Richard sighed. "Go home, son."

The old Monte Carlo roared to life, and Percy flew to Richard's shoulder. He watched as Gene drove away, not proud of scaring the young man.

Fishing a key out of his pocket, he stepped toward his office door. Richard shifted his head, so he could see the bird on his shoulder. He managed a half-smile to his feathered companion as his walked inside and closed the door.

∞

Gene floored the gas pedal in his car, trying to put as many miles between himself and the old maniac and his bird as he could. The voice in his mind returned, this time with a warning. "It's best not to meddle with things you do not understand. Your friend's destiny is written and there is nothing you can do. Stay away from here." Gene shook his head, trying to escape from the skewed reality he found himself.

He thought of calling the local police but knew how fantastic his story would sound. "They'd probably lock me away," he muttered sarcastically. He looked in his rearview mirror, making sure the crow had not managed to wing his way along with him.

Gene took in a long breath and sighed helplessly. All he could do was wait.

Chapter Eight

Saturday, September 22, 2012
One year earlier...

Roger sat on the ground, his body shaking uncontrollably as he cautiously opened his eyes. The blinding light had been replaced with a calm darkness. Blinking his eyes several times, Roger's vision adjusted to the dark and he could see Richard standing a few yards away. Percy sat on the Native's shoulder, staring intently in his direction.

Roger felt something behind his back and realized his large duffel bag had been the culprit of his lack of breath and pain in his ribs. The circle looked as it had, but the weather was warmer, the leaves greener. Richard's hair was up in a ponytail and his clothing had changed.

Roger tried to speak, but his voice was lost in his labored breathing. "Give yourself a moment. You've had a rough trip," Richard grinned as he approached.

He offered Roger his hand and lifted him to his feet.

Roger's legs swayed under him as he tried to regain his sense of equilibrium. Richard steadied him, still smiling at his lack of coordination. "What is your name, son?" Roger's face grew puzzled, not understanding the reason for the question. "I'm Roger Grayson. You know who I am."

The old man laughed faintly, trying to not be completely rude to his new visitor. He replied, "I may yet, or should I say, I will. But this is the first time we have met in my memory." Roger's eyes lit with understanding. "So, I made it? I have really come back in time a year?" "You have come back, but as far as me knowing from what time, I don't. Like I said, this is the first time I have met you," Richard said, his grin growing larger. "So, this is September twenty-second, two thousand twelve?" "It is, son," Richard said as he motioned to the path that ran to the bottom of the hill.

"Follow me to my office and you can tell me all about what brings you here."

Roger nodded and fell in line with Richard as he led the way. Percy had turned to face Roger as he rode on Richard's shoulder. The crow's eyes fixated on his as they made their way down the hill, causing a cold chill to run down his spine. Those unearthly black eyes of the crow triggered a sense of uneasiness throughout his entire body. Percy leapt from Richard's shoulder, causing Roger to throw his hands over his face as the bird came to rest gently on him.

Richard turned slightly, still making his way down the hill. "It just means that he likes you." Roger lowered his hands, looking at his new passenger. "I know; just startled me."

Percy twisted his head from side to side until finally becoming still on Roger's shoulder. He knew the quiet, deep voice he had heard in his head earlier had been Percy's, and it scared the hell out of him. Roger walked woodenly down the rest of the path and the crow flew to the edge of the office's roof. A sigh of relief traversed his dry lips as Richard opened the office door and gestured him to enter.

The gaffer slid behind his desk, retrieved his pipe, and began to clean it. Roger took the seat across from him, his body still shaking from the events of the evening. Richard reached into a pouch sitting next to him and started poking pieces of tobacco into his pipe. "So, Roger, tell me, why has the circle brought you here?"

∞

Lisa busied herself around the Monroe Drugstore, the air catching her white lab coat as she hurried to lock the door. The store should have closed twenty minutes ago, but she had been in the middle of helping Mrs. Van Pelt understand her medicine dosage and didn't want to send her away. Keys in hand, she skidded to a halt at the two glass doors, turning the lock as she looked outside. Mrs. Van Pelt sat in her car, giving Lisa a dainty wave as she drove away.

She walked back to the pharmacy counter and made sure that everything was locked up tight before arming the store's alarm system. Lisa had a spring in her step as she walked over to the lighted keypad and pushed in her security code. A smile crossed her lips as she entered it.

1-3-0-1-9-7-6

It was her fiancé's birthday, the one number she never had issues remembering. Dates and simple life scheduling always seemed to slip through the cracks in her memory. However, Roger was the love of her life, and those numbers were ones she would never forget. Her head was otherwise mostly filled with the chemistry and calculus that had been crammed into it from her university days.

After college, when most of her friends had already married and had kids, Lisa was still waiting for that one guy that would capture her heart. She had moved to Monroe to take the head pharmacist position at the local drugstore. Soon after moving there, a knock at her apartment door opened her life to the man that had occupied her dreams her entire life. He came in the guise of a pizza delivery, carrying her second love, a pepperoni and pineapple with extra cheese.

The security system began beeping its warning to leave the area before it armed, snapping Lisa back to reality. She scurried out the side door, locking it behind her. Walking to her car, her mind fixated on the memory of that half grin which caught her eye nearly a year ago.

Lisa could see Roger standing at her door like it was yesterday, pizza box in hand. Locks of chestnut hair peeked out from underneath his faded baseball cap, his eyes lighting up when she opened the door. Roger tripped over his words as he tried to tell her the total of her order.

Lisa laughed at the memory of his awkward attempt at small talk while she fished for the money in her purse. She handed him the cash in exchange for the warm box which she placed on a table next to the door. He scratched lightly at the back of his neck as she thanked him with a smile and gently closed the door. The following week, Lisa's diet changed from her usual healthful fare to deliveries, just to get a chance to talk to him. After a bit of hint-dropping, Roger got the nerve to ask her out.

The engine purred to life when she turned the key, the slight aroma of exhaust floating into the night air. She pointed her car in the direction of her apartment building as thoughts of her fiancé wiped away all of her day's troubles. "Just one more week!" Lisa squealed to herself.

In just seven days, Lisa would be married to the most perfect human being she had ever met. Just the thought of him sent chills up and down her backbone. The couple had planned a very simplistic wedding ceremony with just a few close friends in attendance.

Neither one of them saw the purpose of breaking the bank on a wedding, especially as Roger had only been at his new job at the library for a few months. Those funds could be used on their future together. A nice, sweet service at a nearby park with lots of flowers, a handful of friends in attendance, and her dress was the extent of their frivolousness.

Lisa's eyes lit up at the thought of her wedding dress. It was the one thing that Roger absolutely refused to cut corners on. It was the most beautiful thing she had ever owned and hugged her figure in all the right places.

She had played out the wedding in her head so many times; it had become the first thing she thought of when she woke up and the last before she fell asleep. Roger completed her life; his mere presence brought a peace to her existence she had never thought possible.

Lisa turned into her apartment complex and parked her car. Gathering her purse, she ran her hand through her hair, pushing it behind her ear as she headed to the door.

Lisa bit her lip slightly, still in her blissful wedding daydream, when she felt a shiver of anticipation building in her chest. She sighed slightly, "Then there's the honeymoon afterward."

∞

Tears in his eyes, Roger watched Richard for any reaction to the story he had just laid before him. He took a puff from his pipe and placed it in the ashtray on his desk. "So, now you know why I have traveled back," Roger stated, waiting for some sort of a reply. Richard nodded, seeming to be lost in thought.

Roger wiped the tears from his burning cheeks. "So, what do you think?" he goaded for an answer. Richard leaned back in his seat. "Well, son, it looks like you have two days to stop your fiancé from being killed in this car wreck." Richard paused for a moment, continuing, "You realize you are going to be here for six months, and you will need a place to stay, transportation, and money."

Roger chimed in, "I have money. That was the one thing I knew I would need. As far as a place to stay, I had thought about staying with my aunt. She lives just outside of Monroe." Richard picked up his pipe, tapped it a few times on the ashtray, and began filling it again. "There's something I have to warn you about. Something that is very important."

Roger leaned forward, making sure he caught every word. "You have to stay away from your past self. It would cause you and everyone you know all sorts of problems." Roger nodded slightly. Richard's face grew solemn, filling with an intensity that Roger had not witnessed. "Son, this is extremely important. Do not, under any circumstances, go looking for your earlier self."

Roger snickered, his voice dripping with sarcasm, "What are you saying, that coming into contact with an earlier version of myself will unravel the fabric of time and destroy the universe?" Richard stopped filling his pipe and stared at Roger, his glare seeming to bore a hole into him.

Roger's blood went cold as Richard sat silently, ignoring his question and replying with his own, "Do you normally visit your aunt?" Roger shook his head.

"How well do you recall the days just before your fiancé's death? Do you remember where you were?" Roger sat back in his chair, trying to remember every detail of the days before her accident. "I spent most of my time working on my house," he recalled.

Intense emotion rocked Roger to his core, as memories of renovating his home came to him in a series of half-forgotten sensations. The texture of the curtains that Lisa had bought for his house, the smell fresh paint filling his nose, and the color of the wood from the new kitchen cabinets that she helped him install; they all nearly overwhelmed him.

Richard seemed to note his sudden sullen mood. "I know remembering this is not easy, but it is vital for you to remember everywhere you went." Roger went silent for another moment as Richard finished loading his pipe, lighting it with a match. He finally replied, "I know that I took her to work the morning of her accident. Other than that, I was either at home or working at the library."

Smoke from Richard's pipe wafted in front of him as he nodded his understanding. "What about a car?" Roger had not thought of that. "I guess I could rent one for a few days, at least until I'm able to prevent the accident." Richard cracked a smile. "There is a car rental shop not far from here, so that should help you out," he paused as he took another draw from his pipe, "as far as you staying with your aunt, that should do for the couple of days you will need in Monroe. The rest of the time I recommend you stay here. I have a place prepared." Roger felt a small shock of surprise at this, haltingly asking, "You...you do?" "Of course," the old man chuckled. "Surely you don't think this is the first time I have assisted in someone's time travel?"

Roger mulled over Richard's words. He never really thought about the wizened Native having dealt with housing time travelers. He broke from his musings in time to hear "I don't need you running around Monroe for six months possibly making things worse than they already are." "I see your point," Roger agreed.

Richard slid an old rotary telephone toward Roger, pointing at a number scrawled on a piece of paper taped to its side. "The number for the car rental is listed here. Call them while I go make sure the spare room is up to par."

Richard stood and walked toward the front door, a trail of smoke following him. Roger lifted the phone's receiver and slowly dialed the number. Before finishing, he turned to Richard's retreating figure. "Thank you for everything. All of this seems just too good to be true."

Richard nodded and let the door close behind him. Roger turned his attention back to the antiquated phone and finished dialing the number. As the phone purred in his ear, the situation settled into Roger's brain, "Maybe it is too good to be true."

Chapter Nine

Richard walked a path around his office, Percy managing to hitch a ride on his shoulder as he made his way to the back of the building. A door was located there that faced the foot of Mystery Hill.

Richard was troubled with his new friend Roger. It had been many seasons since anyone had appeared in the circle. Roger's story had been a complex one, but not all that unusual. He had aided in mending several broken hearts over the years, but he had also seen numerous people return to their normal times in worse condition than they were before they arrived.

Richard took a long draw from his pipe and looked at Percy, giving him a quick rub. The crow leaned into his hand, requesting more attention.

Richard complied, each pass causing the bird to press harder against him.

Percy always knew who to expect through the circle, even if Richard didn't. Richard was fairly certain he even knew the outcome before their arrival.

Richard stopped petting him and unlocked the door to the spare bedroom. The smell of dust and stale air cocooned him as he passed over the threshold. Percy still on his shoulder, he flipped on the light and walked to the room's only window. One good tug later, the smell of fresh, forest air began filling the room. "Cawww!" the bird exclaimed. "There! It shouldn't take but a few minutes for the room to air out."

Richard stepped over to the closet, removing a set of fresh linens and a large, overstuffed pillow, and tossed them on the foot of the bed. The room was sparsely furnished. A small nightstand and lamp sat to the right of the bed. An antique dresser was placed against the wall opposite the bed.

The walls were made of a sweet-smelling cedar, its odor intensified by the air moving in through the open window. He paced back to the window and lowered it, leaving just enough opening for the air to circulate in the room. His thoughts went back to his newly arrived visitor as he walked from the room. "This one worries me, Percy."

∞

Roger twisted in his seat, waiting for Richard to return. He had been able to rent an economy car for a couple of days and not break the bank. Fumbling through his duffel bag, he checked to see that his money had made the trip with him and pulled out the needed cash.

Roger was concerned about Richard's lack of reaction to his reason for travelling back in time. The man seemed like he didn't really care why he was there. Maybe he knew something he wasn't telling. Perhaps it was simply that he had experienced this so many times before, it had become routine for him. Or maybe it was nothing at all. Roger shook the thoughts from his head. There was no reason to continue trying to second guess the man's actions. Time would reveal the truth.

Richard returned to the office, Percy leaping from his arm and onto the roof. Roger could hear the strange bird walking about on the top of the building. Richard had told him more than once that the crow liked him. That knowledge gave him little comfort now.

The Native took his seat behind his desk and looked at Roger pointedly. "Did you manage to get a car?" "Yes. The rental company will be here with it in the morning." "Good. I have the spare room prepared for you. You are welcome to stay here, out of sight, until March, which is when I can send you back to your own time. Just keep in mind: you have two days to complete your task." "My task?" Roger thought to himself. He did not like how nonchalant Richard was about the whole affair. Richard lit his pipe. "If you will follow the path around the building, the first door you come to leads into your room."

Roger stood up and offered his hand to the old man, saying, "Thank you for everything you have done. If it wasn't for you, I would not be able to see my Lisa again." Richard smiled, his pipe between his teeth, and gave Roger's hand a firm shake. "I'm glad to be of service to you." Richard let go of his hand, adding, "Just remember, stay away from your other self."

He nodded his understanding, picked up his duffel, and turned to leave.

"Good night." The old man nodded, and Roger stepped out the door, scratching his head. "What is wrong with him? He acts as though he really doesn't give a shit," he mumbled under his breath.

Roger rounded the corner of the building, seeing the door to his room. He could hear a small tapping sound just above him and realized that Percy was on the roof, following his every move. Pausing before entering the door, he stared intently at the crow. "You know what's going on, don't you Percy?" "Cawww!"

He stepped inside his room, threw his duffel bag on the bed, and settled himself next to it. Roger looked at his watch and released a confused, irritated sigh. "Tomorrow can't get here soon enough."

∞

Lisa lay in her bed, her head full of the plans for her wedding day. She couldn't sleep. Her anticipation of the upcoming event had turned a butterfly collection loose in her stomach.

A smile came across her lips as she imagined Roger standing at the center of the park, the sun casting a glow upon him, and the minister just behind him. Every step she would take down the aisle towards him brought her one moment closer to being next to the man of her dreams.

Lisa tossed in her bed, her body tingling with excitement as she thought of Roger's lips meeting hers. She shifted underneath her sheets, hugged her pillow tightly, and buried her face deep into it. Her imagination grabbed Roger tight and held him snuggly to her body.

Lisa sighed and kicked her feet in a restless spasm. Sleep would not be finding her tonight. Her brain was too full of work mixed with wedding plans.

She rolled over onto her belly and pulled her body pillow over her head, another muffled sigh sneaking from her lips. Lisa peered out a small opening between her pillow and the bed, eyeballing the clock on her nightstand. "Gah...two-thirty in the morning." Their wedding day couldn't come soon enough.

∞

Roger stared at the ceiling of Richard's extra room, wishing his mind would give him a bit of peace. He had played a dozen different scenarios over in his head about how the next two days would unfold. He'd follow each one to their ultimate conclusion, some ending with happily ever after, some with ultimate ruin.

One fact was completely clear. In less than two days Lisa would be dead unless he was able to prevent it. If he prevented her death, they would be married in about a week. He had one chance to stop her from being killed. The question was how to do it.

Roger knew from Richard's warnings to avoid contact with his past self. He had to let Lisa be taken to work on Monday morning. He also knew that at some point her dad would pick up her car at her apartment and drop it off while she was at work.

One of the scenarios Roger considered was to somehow disable her car before she could drive home. That way she could never get into the accident. Lisa would be getting off work around six o'clock, so he had to get there before that time. He wasn't worried about running into himself while she was at the drugstore because his other self was at home painting.

Maybe it wouldn't take something as extreme as messing with her car. Maybe simply going and seeing her at work, delaying her leaving would be enough. The only problem with that would be that she might question his other self about his visit at the drugstore, causing trouble between the two of them later. Roger's head began to hurt as he went over all the things that could go wrong.

One thing he knew for certain, he had to go to his Aunt Tela's house in the morning. Once there, he could make the ultimate decision on how to delay Lisa leaving work.

Roger rolled onto his side, facing the room's window. He could see movement outside, which made his heart skip a beat. Was he being watched?

He slipped from his bed and crept to the opening. All he could see was the moonlight. The wind from outside caused an uncontrollable quake to course down his spine and settle into his toes. Roger reached for the window and slid it closed.

He turned toward his bed and a loud thump echoed from the window, causing him to spin around and fall to his knees. Terror washed over his body, fear locking his eyes on the small window. He could hear something just outside, but it was too low to see out of the glass.

Roger slid himself across the floor, keeping low so not to be seen. He reached the wall and cautiously rose from his crouched position. The tangy flavor of fear stung the back of his throat; horrified at what he might see when he made it to his feet.

He placed his hands on the window sill and thrust himself upward. A black shadow passed the opening and another loud thump sent him back to the hard floor.

Roger felt as if his heart was going to pound out of his chest when a familiar eye caught his gaze from behind the glass. He gasped with surprise and then ran his hand across his forehead, removing the sweat that streamed toward his eyes.

Percy stood on the window's ledge, occasionally glancing in while pacing back and forth. Roger wrapped his arms around himself and produced a laugh that stung his own ears. "Percy! You scared the shit out of me!" The crow pecked at the ledge and peered back inside, "Cawww!"

The bird flew away, and Roger crawled back into his bed. He closed his eyes, waiting for his pulse to slow to a normal beat. Roger put his hand over his face, releasing a long, irritated sigh. "I'm never going to fall asleep now."

Chapter Ten

Sunday, September 23, 2012

The next morning, Roger stood at the foot of his bed, organizing his belongings in the duffel bag. He had packed in such a hurry he wasn't quite sure what clothes he'd managed to toss into it.

He rubbed his eyes, trying to rid himself of the dull burn growing in his head from lack of sleep. His thoughts of Percy and last night were still branded in his brain. A knock came from the door, causing him to start at the sound.

The door opened a crack; Richard's voice emanated from the fissure. "Roger, your rental car is here." Retrieving his bag from the bed, Roger walked to the door and opened it the rest of the way. Richard stood there, with Percy assuming his usual resting place on his shoulder.

Roger glared at the crow, a familiar wave of fear washing over him. He began to wonder if the bird was some sort of malevolent force and not the friendly spirit he had once believed him to be.

He turned his attention to his guide. "Thank you for coming to let me know." Roger quickly walked away from the two, not liking the vibe in the air.

Richard fell in step behind him. "Have you got everything you need?" Not turning to speak, Roger quickly thought of an answer. "As far as I know. There's not much I need, other than food and clothes. I'm sure my aunt will make sure I'm well looked after."

"So, you will be returning after you have prevented the accident?" Roger reached the rental car and turned to face him. "That is my plan," he lied. Richard halted, causing Roger to wonder if the elder had some ability to detect falsehoods. "If your plans change, you will let me know? You will have to come back here in order for me to return you to your proper time." Roger managed a grin. "I will let you know."

Richard offered his hand and Roger returned the gesture with hesitation. He took another look at Percy, questioning what was brewing in his little bird mind.

Richard opened the door on the gold Chevrolet Spark. "Be careful in your travels. I hope that your wishes are fulfilled." Roger tossed the bag into the passenger's seat and slid into the driver's seat. He gave the old fellow a nod. "She is all that matters to me. It would be pointless to try to explain just how much I love Lisa."

Richard stepped back, speaking again with an authoritative tone. "Now you understand why you had the capability to transverse time to be where you are now." Roger looked up, bewildered. "I don't understand." Richard nodded, a slight smile dancing in his eyes. "Not everyone can do what you accomplished yesterday. The strength of your love is what gave you the power to survive the time-bridge. Without that love within you, none of this would have been possible."

Percy leaned toward Roger and lowered his head for him to pet. He reached for him and gave his black feathers a quick stroke, still leery of the animal.

Richard continued, "Love of the intensity that lives within you is something I rarely witness; it burns stronger than any star in the heavens. Just don't let it consume you."

Roger turned the key in the ignition, the car roaring to life. "I will try my best." With that, he drove away,

Richard and Percy disappearing in his rearview mirror.

∞

Richard watched Roger's car fade into the morning light. He turned back to his office door, petting his dark friend as he walked. "Do you think we'll see him again, Percy?" The bird remained silent and repositioned his head, requesting Richard to rub under his beak.

Richard gave Percy a half smile and ran his weathered hand along his friend's throat before stepping into his office. Percy jumped from his shoulder to land on a nearby perch.

Richard sat in his chair, fished out his pouch of tobacco, and began loading his pipe. "Percy, I'm not so sure about this one. I've never sensed such an abyss of vulnerability like what's trapped in that boy's soul."

Percy bobbed his head and began cleaning his feathers. Smoke engulfed Richard as he lit his pipe. "I fear we may not see him again."

∞

Roger tried, with little success, to convince himself he had nothing to fear from Richard and his crow. He had little intention of returning to Mystery Hill until he had to depart for his proper time. Percy, who had once given him a sense of peace, now filled him with dread.

He cleared his throat, trying to distract his thoughts and occupied his mind with visiting his aunt. It had been a long time since he had paid her a visit, and with good reason. The woman was cantankerous as hell, and that was a compliment to her demeanor.

Roger had many childhood memories of her, standing on her front porch with a large broom in her hand. Many times, his backside had met that broom if he stepped out of line. He always hated going to her house, but his mother had insisted he visit her at least once a year.

His aunt was a formidable woman, even more so after his uncle had left her after a few years of marriage. They never had any children, which further complicated matters for Roger and his cousins that would endure summertime exiles from their parents at her home. She had no experience relating to kids.

Roger had seen her a few years ago and it seemed that old age had mellowed her a bit. If there were any place in the world that would be safe for him to stay and not run into his past self, it was Aunt Tela's house.

Roger returned to concentrating on the road, placing the memories of his aunt in the back of his mind. "I should be in Manchester in a few minutes. It's time for me to find some food."

∞

Lisa rolled over in her bed, her eyes catching the time on her alarm clock. She bolted from her bed, blankets flying wild. "I've overslept!" She rushed into the bathroom, tossing her clothes as she jumped into the shower.

Every Sunday morning, she and Roger would meet at the park. It had become a tradition ever since their first date. She twisted the knob to the shower, the water cascading over her body.

As she stood under the water to wet her long hair, the memory of the park took over her thoughts. She could still remember the day Roger placed his hand under her chin, turning her head toward him. The warm water from the shower mimicked the force that discharged through her body as his lips met hers. The memory of their first kiss sent the familiar twinges down her spine, landing a few inches below her belly button.

Lisa took the bar of soap from the shelf on the shower's wall and scrubbed it into a washcloth. She started with her neck, rubbing the cloth just below her ears. The sensation was reminiscent of Roger kissing about her neck and shoulders. She blinked her eyes back to reality, blushing at where her mind was going.

"Okay, okay...calm down, Lisa," she said to herself, a mischievous grin forming on her lips. She finished her shower, retrieving an oversized towel from its rack. The towel was soft like satin as she dried herself and then wrapped it around her body.

Lisa looked in the mirror and stuck her tongue out at her reflection. For most of her life, she'd rarely felt attractive. Since meeting Roger, however, she felt like the most beautiful woman in the world.

She always took special care when fixing her hair. It was the one thing, aside from her eyes, that Roger constantly commented on. To her, it was just a brown mop. To Roger, it was something for him to run his fingers through over and over again. It would always set her body on fire.

Picking up the blow dryer, she switched it on and began brushing her hair's length, the warm air passing by her ear now and again. The recollection of Roger's warm kisses on her lobes flooded her senses; his tongue circling her ear.

Lisa caught her refection in the mirror and realized she was merely standing there with her dryer in one hand, her brush in the other; her work was lost in the clouds of her imagination. She shook her head a bit and went back to work.

After finishing her hair, she started on her makeup, with great emphasis on her eyes. She loved how Roger would fixate on them, his face softening as he stared deep into her soul. Eyeing a piece of jewelry by her bathroom mirror, she slid on a beautiful white gold bracelet. It was the first gift that Roger had ever given her and was her most valued possession.

Lisa dashed from the bathroom to her closet. She shifted the hangers to and fro, looking for one of her favorite outfits. "Ah ha! There you are!" She grabbed up the green top and hurried into the bedroom.

Taking another look at the clock, she rushed to get dressed. She didn't want to keep him waiting. She loved Roger and could never envision her future without him at her side. Lisa believed herself to be half of a soul before she met her little pizza delivery man. Roger made her complete.

∞

Roger greeted the signs that read variations of *Welcome to Manchester* with a nod. It had seemed like an eternity since he had eaten. He could hear his stomach lodging a protest as he pulled his car into the Drive-In on Valley Street. "Just something quick," he mused

He stopped his car just in front of the plain white building and walked quickly to the order window, surprised not to encounter its usual line. A perky face appeared, requesting his order.

"I'd like a lobster roll with onion rings and a large chocolate malted. Oh, and do you have fried mushrooms?" There was a short pause and the youth returned with, "No sir." "That's okay, then." She gave him the total, he thanked her and returned to wait in the car while his order was prepared.

"Shame, I loved their mushrooms," he mumbled. He reached over to the radio and started thumbing through the different stations, stopping at one of his favorite songs, *Hey*, *Soul Sister*, by Train. "Lisa and I heard this on the radio at the park," Roger recalled. Soon after that day at the park, they had dubbed it 'their song'. He drummed his fingers to the beat of the music, losing himself in the song's lyrics.

∞

Lisa drove up McIndoes Falls Road, leading toward the Connecticut River. Today, like every Sunday, her excitement was building at the thought of seeing Roger at the park. Most of her friends thought her nuts for meeting him every weekend at the river. She would always brush off their teasing and return with a sarcastic retort, "You are just jealous your boyfriend doesn't have a picnic with you once a week." It was all in good fun. Her friends knew their love was special, and Lisa knew they probably were a little bit jealous of it.

She leaned toward the mirror and checked her makeup once more as she approached their spot by the river. Roger's car sat where it always did, just at the water's edge. Stopping her car next to his, she could see him meandering about, getting everything ready for her.

He looked up at her arrival and walked toward her car. She jumped out and met him with a bear hug and several small kisses all around his face. "I'm sorry that I'm late." Roger held onto her hips but pulled back just enough to look into her eyes. "It's okay," he replied, smiling. "It gave me time to get the blanket and all the goodies out before you got here."

He took a long look at her green button up top and close-fitting jeans. "You are absolutely hot, you know that?" Lisa blushed at his words and returned, "No, you are!" Roger winked at her, noting her rosy cheeks and motioned toward the blanket at the side of the river.

They always took turns bringing the food for their Sunday get-together. Roger would always try to find something unusual to bring, just to see if she would eat it. So far, nothing had been too strange. They started to turn, and Roger seemed to stare at her car for a moment.

"What is it? "she asked, wondering what pulled his attention away. He bent down and examined one of her car's tires. "Looks like you need to get some new treads soon. This one is looking for kind of bald." Lisa looked at the tire and nodded. "Yeah, you're right. I'll give my dad a call tomorrow and let him know." She added a hint of sarcastic mischief to her voice, "He knows a guy."

Roger smiled at her mocking tone. "Oh, he knows a guy. This guy an expert on rubber or something?" Roger taunted back. Lisa wrapped her arm in his as they walked toward the blanket. "Maybe," she grinned.

Their entire relationship, they had been ridiculously silly with each other. It made Lisa love him all the more. Roger's odd ability to make her laugh, even when she didn't feel like it, calmed her in a way she had never thought possible. She tried to do the same for him.

The two of them sat on the blanket and Lisa started burrowing through the basket to see what sort of food he had brought to test out on her this time. "Be careful!" Roger warned. Lisa drew her hands back, looking at him with serious concern. "Why?" "They might get out," he grinned.

She looked back at the basket, wondering just exactly what was in there. "They?" "The snails," he replied, trying to hide his mirth. "I thought you might like to try some escargot this week." Lisa glared at him in disgust. "You're joking? Right?"

His eyes met hers and she could see he was doing everything possible not to burst into tremendous laughter. Roger shook his head. "Yes, I'm joking. But you should have seen the look on your face!" He couldn't hold it in anymore. The laughter came pouring out of him in waves.

Lisa leaned over to pop him in the arm and was met with Roger's lips against hers. They both rolled onto their sides, arms wrapped around each other's body. He finally broke the kiss. "You really think I would feed my baby snails?" She bit her lip then smiled, saying, "I don't know. You have brought some really strange things in that basket before." They both giggled before locking their lips together again, kissing for several minutes before Lisa pulled her mouth away. "I love you, Roger. More than anything."

∞

The young order taker tapped at Roger's car window. "Sir? Your order's been ready for a while." He nodded and followed her back to the window. She handed him a bag and his drink in exchange for his proffered money and turned away.

After returning to the car, Roger looked at the food sitting at the bottom of the bag, then to the radio. The song that played earlier had twisted his stomach into a thousand knots. He sat his food in the passenger's seat next to his duffel and cranked the car to leave. "I'm not so hungry anymore."

Chapter Eleven

Roger continued on his journey to Aunt Tela's house. He had debated on calling before he arrived, but even if he did, her welcome would be forced at best. She lived in a little brick house just south of Monroe and rarely had visitors.

As Roger drove up the long driveway, a feeling of doom settled on him. It was the same sensation he remembered feeling when he was six years old. He parked his car under the same old oak tree that his mom parked under and glared at the house. It hadn't changed much over the years; it still scared the hell out of him. The concrete porch was the same dull blue-gray and a white metal railing still circled its edge.

Roger reached for the car's door handle, slowly opened it, and stepped from the car. It felt as if his feet were dragging through molasses as he approached the front steps. He stood at the old screen door and took a long, deep breath before knocking, the metal screen rattling in its frame.

Several seconds went by, then a minute. She had to be home. She never went anywhere. Roger knocked again. The wooden door on the other side of the screen flew open revealing a woman in her mid-sixties, around five feet tall with long salt and pepper hair. The frown on her face looked as though it was permanently etched into her leathery skin.

The old woman adjusted her glasses and glared at Roger, barking "Who are you?" Her voice brought horrible flashbacks to the surface of Roger's brain. "It's me, Aunt Tela." She adjusted her glasses again. "Roger? Oh, I didn't recognize you." Her empty reply fell lifeless in the air.

Roger cleared his throat and began the conversation he had rehearsed on his way here, "I haven't seen you in a long time. I wondered if you would mind if I visited with you for a day or so." Aunt Tela just looked at him through her coke bottle thick rimmed glasses. "Well, don't just stand out here on the porch. Come inside." Roger smirked a bit, realizing that was her way of saying it was okay for him to stay.

As he walked to the living room, all the familiar sights and smells overwhelmed him. The house had not changed in at least twenty-five years. Everything still as it was. The only visible difference being a color television that had replaced her old black and white set. As far as the smell, Roger could never figure out exactly what it was. It was a cross between mothballs and old socks.

He took a seat on the plastic covered couch with his aunt sitting across from him in her antique chair. The silence in the room was eating at him as he tried to think of something to say. Something finally came to mind. "I see you have gotten a new television since I was here."

"Yeah, the other one went out on me. Got that one about three years ago." "Do you like it?" Roger quizzed. "I just use it to watch the news and the weather. Not much of anything good on TV these days."

Roger started to feel the sweat forming in his palms. The old woman turned her watery gaze on him. "So, what brings you out here, Roger? You've not been out here in a long time. If I didn't ask your mother about you, I'd think you fell of the face of the earth." Roger fidgeted, trying to think of a good explanation. "Oh, you know. Working at the library keeps me pretty busy." Aunt Tela grunted and continued, "Your mother tells me you are getting married soon. Not getting cold feet are ya?"

His aunt's remark pricked deep into his heart. He attempted to reply gently, "Not at all. Lisa is the best thing that ever happened to me. She makes me truly happy." Aunt Tela pushed her glasses up on her nose. "Humph! Marriage isn't going to bring you happiness. You best be looking for it somewhere else."

Anger burned behind Roger's eyes. He bit the inside of his cheek, trying to fight off the urge to curse out his aunt and storm out the door. It didn't help that he had already lost Lisa in the accident, but now he had to listen to his aunt badmouth a marriage that never got to happen.

Roger interrupted his aunt's continued muttering about the idiocy of joining yourself to another person, saying, "She's a really sweet girl, Aunt T."

"Ha!" Tela snorted. "I give the marriage two years, three at most. That's how long mine..."

Roger jumped to his feet and erupted in rage; a rage that had built up over his entire life against his bitter older family member. "Listen, you crazy old witch! Just because your marriage fell apart doesn't mean mine will! I have gone great lengths to make this work with Lisa; something that you would never understand!" Roger took a deep breath, his face purple with disgust. "So, you can stay here locked up in your house, alone and miserable, but you aren't going to make me miserable with you!"

With that, Roger stormed from the house, the metal screen door slamming as he flew out the doorway. He leapt into his rental car and made a U-turn in his aunt's driveway, cursing under his breath the whole time.

Roger's labored breathing echoed in his ears. "Now what am I going to do? Where am I going to stay?" His mind raced at the possibilities available to him, which were few.

He could stay with one of his friends. No, he couldn't do that because it could cause trouble for him in the future. How could he explain being in two places at once? He could always sleep in his car, as unpleasant as that would be. An idea came to him. He could drive down to the park by the Connecticut River and sleep in his car there.

Roger had not been to the park since Lisa's accident. He'd not been able to visit without her but knowing that she was alive at this point in time would make the atmosphere not quite so morbid. At night, people rarely visited the park, so he hoped he wouldn't be bothered.

Roger's head swam with so much he had to decide. He was near the point of overload. His biggest issue was he still had not decided exactly how he was going to prevent Lisa's accident. He directed his car northwest toward the river, praying he made the right decision. His time and Lisa's were soon to run out.

∞

Lisa returned to her apartment after a wonderful day at the river. Her cheeks were still pink with happiness from the time she had spent with Roger. She stepped into the bathroom and began undressing, her thoughts turning to how it felt to have Roger's hands on her body.

She slid her top over her head and then reached for her wrist to remove her bracelet. A gasp left her lips when the white gold wristlet was not resting where it should have been. Lisa frantically looked around the bathroom, trying to find the beautiful gift that Roger had given her months ago.

She slid her top back on and followed her every step through the apartment, but no bracelet was to be found. "Oh God, please tell me I haven't lost it!" She went back to her car and looked inside.

Nothing.

Sliding upright in her seat, she started her car and headed back to the park in hopes of finding her lost gift.

∞

Roger pulled his car into its usual parking spot at the park. It felt so odd being back at the river's edge again. It had grown dark outside, but he debated on getting out and looking around. He just sat there, his chin resting on the steering wheel, and stared out on the water.

He had really missed the place. Roger rolled down his window and flipped on the radio, setting the mood that he would have set for Lisa before her accident.

Taking a deep breath, the scent of the water and freshly cut grass filled his nostrils. He leaned back in his seat and closed his eyes to imagine his beautiful love. For the first time in nearly a year he felt calm and at peace.

His serene moment was quickly interrupted as a flicker of light caught his eye in the rearview mirror, causing him to slide down in his seat. "Great! I was hoping no one would be out here tonight," he protested.

A car pulled in just beside him, though he could not see who was in it due to his shrunken position. He heard a door open, and someone step out onto the pavement. After several seconds, he rose from his slumped location in the car.

Roger recognized the make and model of the vehicle to be the same as Lisa's. "Oh shit!" He hissed as he slid back low in his seat. He tried to be completely still until he realized he was holding his breath. Taking in more air, he started to inhale and exhale a normal rhythm.

What was Lisa doing here at this time of night? He rose up again, just enough to peer though the bottom of the window. It was Lisa alright. Her work badge and name tag were in view hanging from her car's mirror.

Roger's mind raced at what to do. "Should I go talk to her? Should I stay where I am? God, I just want to see her and hold her again!" His thoughts finally hit overload as he struggled to make the right choice.

A single tear rolled down his cheek. Lisa was so near him and he knew that even speaking to her could be the worst thing he could do. His hand itched to pull the door handle, leap from his car, and scoop her into his arms. Even after a year, he could still feel her wet lips against his, her tongue tracing the borders of his mouth.

He froze in place as he heard her approaching her car. "God help me, what do I do?" Roger heard her car door open and close. He barely caught a glimpse of her as she backed out and drove away.

He grabbed his steering wheel, banging his forehead into its bottom. Tears coursed down his cheeks as he gritted his teeth, saliva forming at the corners of his mouth. His eyelids were squeezed so tightly, his eyes burned like fire had coursed through his pupils. "She was right there! God in heaven, she was just outside my car!"

Roger's weeping began to overpower him, his insides pumping like a churn with each breath. He grabbed for the door handle just in time to heave his belly's contents onto the pavement. His sobbing increased and what words did pass his lips were completely unintelligible.

Roger started taking long, deep breaths, trying to prevent himself from hyperventilating. He reached into his Drive-In bag and removed a couple of napkins, first drying his eyes and then wiping his entire face. At this point he really didn't care where he slept. He started up his car and sped away, tossing out the soiled napkins as he went.

Roger's mind was made up. The first motel he passed, that was where he would stay. He had enough money for at least one night. It would give him time to clean up, find something to eat, and make his final decision on how to stop Lisa's accident.

∞

Lisa arrived back at home with her usual smile back on her lips. She had found her bracelet sitting on one of the benches at the park, still confused how it got there.

Her teeth wrapped around her bottom lip. "It must have been when Roger was kissing me and pushed me down on the bench," she decided, a devious sparkle in her eyes. Lisa could never get enough of Roger's affections. He never failed to cause floods of pleasure every time he touched her.

She finished undressing just in time for her phone to ring. Sighing as she picked up the receiver, she was greeted by her father's voice. "Hey daddy," she chimed.

"I got your message about your car needing new tires. I talked to my friend Patrick, and he said I could bring it by in the morning and he would fix you up." Lisa sighed, saying, "Dad, you don't have to do that. You are busy enough with work."

Her father's voice took on his mocking 'I'm the boss' tone. "No arguments young lady. Mom and I will come by your apartment in the morning to pick up your car and have it back to you at the drugstore before your shift ends." Lisa sighed and smiled. "Okay, dad. There's never any point in arguing with you about anything, especially if it has to do with cars."

"Wow! It's only taken you thirty-three years to figure that out," he laughed. Lisa returned his laughter. "Ha ha! I'll see you in the morning, dad. I love you." "I love you too, sweetheart. I'll call you in the morning."

With that, Lisa hung up the phone and quickly called Roger to remind him she needed a ride to work in in the morning. She finished getting ready for bed and snuggled under her warm blankets. Lisa smiled one last time before she fell asleep. "Maybe I'll dream of Roger tonight."

∞

Lisa lay in her bed; her blankets snugly wrapped around her like a cocoon. She heard someone enter her bedroom, but the sound didn't cause her any fear. A warm pair of lips met hers and she returned the touch with a slight moan.

There was no doubt it was Roger's mouth that had encountered hers. She ran her tongue along the boundary of his sweet lips, causing his tongue to meet hers in a synchronized dance within her mouth. He eased himself under her sheets and comforter, kissing the length of her body, his warm breath sending waves of pleasure to every part of her.

She felt her panties slide off her hips, down her legs, and disappearing at her toes. He ran his lips along the inside of her thigh, causing her to cry out slightly and her back to arch.

A gentle hand rubbed over the wetness between her legs, his fingers finding just the right spot with a circular motion. Lisa bit her lip as his other hand slid inside, her body wrapping tightly around him.

She could feel the intense pleasure welling up inside of her, pleading to be released in one massive wave. Between her breathy moans she begged, "Please, go inside me. Come in me."

His hands quickly slid from her body, and she felt the length of him glide into her. Lisa cried out, the pleasure being almost too much to bear. She felt herself letting go as her body quivered with each orgasm, her pleasure-filled screams ringing in her ears.

Roger moaned in ecstasy as she felt him spill himself inside of her, each thrust of his body sending a shockwave to her very core. He slumped forward and rested his head on her breast.

She reached up and ran her fingers through his hair, tugging with each pass. Lisa smiled in absolute contentment and finally opened her eyes to look into his.

Roger wasn't there.

Lisa opened her eyes wider and looked around the room, blushing a bit, but still smiling none the less. "It was a dream," she said out loud. She cuddled back up in the comforter, her legs slightly quaking from the experience. Lisa bit her lip and mused, "He truly is a dream come true."

∞

Roger had found what his mother might call "a rinky-dink motel" just on the outskirts of Monroe to stay for the night. It was twenty bucks a day and after going into the room, he saw why.

The carpets were matted down, the small refrigerator was broken, and the television, he could have sworn, was the same old black and white model set his Aunt Tela used to own.

He examined the bathroom to find one of the pipes had leaked onto the floor, only stopping because someone had turned off the valve underneath. Luckily, the shower still worked, but the shower curtain was little more than a giant plastic bag hanging from a metal rod.

It was of little concern to him. At least the water was warm, and he took the time to shower. Roger couldn't exactly recall the last time he had bathed.

After drying himself, he inspected the bed. It looked as though the mattress was at least thirty years old. The comforter looked equally as antiquated. He pulled the comforter back to see the condition of the sheets. They were probably the newest thing in the whole room. That or someone had used some really powerful bleach.

He dressed himself with the one set of pajamas he'd managed to toss in his duffel bag. Roger slid under the cold, clammy pair of sheets and kicked the comforter to the floor. It was bad enough to look at; he really didn't want it touching him.

As he tried to settle himself, Roger realized he still hadn't eaten. The food he'd bought at the Drive-In sat untouched in his rental car. Eating seemed of little importance. The normal hunger pangs had not hit him since that morning, but he made a mental note he needed to find something to eat on waking.

Checking the alarm clock to make sure that it worked, he set the time for eight in the morning. He had calculated leaving the motel soon after that should give him time to get to Lisa's apartment and do what he needed to do.

Roger had decided on a plan, he just prayed to God that it would work.

Chapter Twelve

Monday, September 24, 2012

Lisa had readied herself for work and stood on her apartment's balcony, waiting for Roger. Still groggy, she stifled a yawn as the sun's rays beamed on her from the east. She checked her lab coat to see that her badge and name tag were in her pocket, giving it a reassuring pat.

Per her dad's instructions, she'd left her car key under the floor mat so that he could retrieve it and take it to his friend. Lisa stared out toward the horizon and saw Roger's blue Honda Civic travel around the curve to her apartment's parking lot.

She made her way down the stairs and met Roger as he pulled into the lot. "Need a lift gorgeous?" His tone dripped with its usual playful sarcasm. Lisa leaned toward his open passenger window and smirked, "I don't know. How far you going?" Roger snickered under his breath. "As far as you let me, princess."

Opening the door, she landed in Roger's passenger seat and leaned toward him, her lips only an inch from his. "Take me to the moon and back." Roger caught her lips and placed his hand behind her head to caress her hair as they kissed.

Lisa broke the kiss and lightly smacked him on the leg. "Come on you, I'm going to be late." He smiled a big, toothy grin as he pressed the gas petal. "Yes ma'am."

Leaving the parking lot, Roger inquired, "Your dad got a key to your car?" Lisa shook her head. "No, he told me to just leave the key under the mat." "Okay, just making sure."

Lisa wrapped her arms around one of his as they made their way to the drug store. Her heart was overflowing with happiness. Roger always looked out for her. She knew it wasn't him treating her like a child. It was simply his way of making sure she would be okay. With Roger, Lisa knew she would be forever safe in his arms.

∞

The alarm in Roger's motel buzzed with a strained chime, telling him it was time to get to it. His eyes rolled in their sockets as he reached over and punched the off button. Roger had slept like a dead man due to the events of the last twenty-four hours. So much had happened in such a short time.

He shoved the sheets away from his body as he twisted his frame so that his feet landed on the floor. His stomach reminded him that his first order of business was to eat, and soon.

Roger got dressed, tucked his pajamas in his bag, and made one final survey of the room before giving it a small salute and closing the door. After placing his key in the drop box at the cashier's window, he unlocked his gold Chevy Spark and flopped into its seat.

Roger may have slept like the dead, but he felt like the dead too. Driving off toward town, he stopped by a doughnut shop drive-through and ordered a half dozen and a large water. He had little concern for the taste of the food and drink. He just needed something to stop his stomach's protesting. Roger gobbled down the six lumps of fried dough and finished off the water in route to his destination, Lisa's apartment.

Over the past day, Roger had come up with what he considered a viable plan. He knew that Lisa's car key was in her car. The best way to keep her out of the accident would be to simply hide her car to where she couldn't drive it. His biggest concern was getting to it before her father came to pick it up, and then where to hide it.

Roger's plan was to take her car across the state line into Vermont, which was just west of Monroe. The next city had begun clearing for a new subdivision project. The region was mainly wooded area, and he hoped there would be enough cover to conceal the car until some of the workers accidentally happened upon it.

His biggest fear was being seen, because most of the people around Lisa's apartment knew who he was. They wouldn't question his presence, but he'd rather not have eyewitnesses pointing out they saw him in Lisa's stolen vehicle.

Bringing his car around a curve, he could see Lisa's apartment come into view. His mouth went dry as he thought of what he was about to do. He'd never stolen anything in his life.

He slid his rental car in on one end of the parking lot, hoping it would not be immediately noticed among all the other vehicles. Roger's nerves were completely frayed, but it was necessary to save his fiancé's life.

He turned off his car and dashed for Lisa's just a few car lengths away. He opened the door, slipped his hand under the floor mat, and retrieved the key. Roger could hear his heart drumming away in his ears as he turned the key in the ignition.

The car came to life, and he thrust it into reverse to make his way out of the lot. His hands stuck to the steering wheel from the sweat oozing from his pores. He slowed as he approached the exit and calmly steered it onto the main road.

He quickly wiped the beads of sweat from his brow, checking all his mirrors to see if anyone was around that might have noticed him leave.

As he maneuvered the curve from the apartment, Roger's pulse double-timed as another car passed him going the opposite direction. "Shit!" His vision went nearly white in fear and his blood could be heard like thick molasses churning through his veins. It was Lisa's father.

All of Roger's senses intensified as he jammed his foot on the accelerator. The car lurched forward, its speed doubling as he reached the western part of Monroe. He couldn't tell if her father had recognized him or the car, but he assumed he knew it was his daughter's vehicle he'd just passed on the highway.

Roger was a few miles out of town as he coasted over the bridge that spanned the Connecticut River. As he entered Vermont, a traffic light in front of him turned a glowing red. He had no intention of stopping.

Pressing the gas pedal hard, he rocketed through the intersection just in time to see a Vermont State Patrol car slide behind him from the other roadway. Roger was beyond terrified, his entire body soaked in perspiration.

He floored the gas again, frantically trying to get to the new subdivision to rid himself of Lisa's car. He saw the blue lights flash in his mirror and could hear the sounds of the police siren slowly get louder and louder.

He tried one last effort to get away from the cop, topping a speed of one hundred miles an hour. Another patrol car cut in front of him blocking his way.

Roger slammed on his breaks, putting the car to a sideways skid as it stopped at the road's edge. It was over.

Roger was completely void of feeling as one of the officers opened the door and threw him to the gravel beside the road. He could hear the muffled voices of the policeman screaming at him, but the words meant nothing to him. His senses had totally shut down.

Roger felt a slight bite of metal against his wrists as one of the officers handcuffed him and tossed him into his patrol car.

Chapter Thirteen

Roger lay on a small, padded cot in the Barnet City Jail. He couldn't even open his eyes to look outside his cell. He was too worried about what to do next. His own stupidity swam throughout him. His lack of planning weighed heavily on his heart, its beat fueling the obsession to save his fiancé's life.

His cheeks were still smeared with blood from having his face ground into the pavement during his arrest. The slightest tear trails were visible from where he had silently wept while in his cell.

For all Roger knew, Lisa would be dead in a few hours. The police would tell him nothing. In return, he did the same. He had no identification on him. He had accidentally left everything in the duffel bag in the rental car.

All the police knew was who the car he had been driving belonged to. Roger was originally told he had been arrested for reckless endangerment, but later was informed he also had another charge of grand theft auto. He refused to give his name in fear it would get back to Lisa. Any way he looked at it, his relationship with his fiancé was completely screwed.

Roger heard the steel door to the main hall of the jail open; a pair of footsteps headed in his direction. He hid his face in case it was someone coming to identify him. The footsteps stopped at his cell. Silence enveloped him for at least a minute before a familiar voice reverberated in his ears. "Looks like you've gone and made a mess of everything, haven't you son?"

Roger bolted to his feet, the old Native's voice bringing hope into his heart again. "Richard! How the hell did you know I was here?" He grinned back at Roger from the other side of the steel bars, and replied "How do you think I knew?"

Roger shrugged. His smile slowly faded as he intoned, "Percy told me. He knew you'd get in trouble, as did I." Roger rested his head against the bars next to his cot, defeated. "I don't know what else to do, Richard. I don't even know where Lisa is right now."

"She's still at work," Richard assured him, "but not for long. The police returned her car to her father. You have just enough time to get to her before the accident."

Roger threw his hands wide. "Well, as you can see, I'm not going anywhere." Richard beamed a big toothy smile at Roger. "Yes, you are. I bailed you out. I just wanted to talk to you before they let you out."

The old man motioned toward one of the guards at the end of the hall and he slowly made his way to Roger's jail cell. The guard opened the door and Roger stepped out, still confused about the whole affair. "You mean I'm free to go?" The guard nodded and stepped away, going back to his station.

Richard rested his hand on Roger's shoulder. "Come on. You've got work to do."

∞

Lisa stood behind the counter at Monroe's Drugstore and listened to her father, David, explain what had happened to her car while she'd been at work. Her jaw dropped in disbelief. "So, you'll telling me that some unknown guy stole my car from outside my apartment, headed to Vermont with it, and got caught because he ran a traffic light?"

David nodded in response. "That's crazy!" Lisa exclaimed, a bit too loud, causing her lone customer to visibly start. She smiled apologetically. Her father continued, "If I hadn't passed him on the road to your apartment, they may not have made the connection and returned your car as fast as they did."

Lisa shook her head at how surreal the story sounded. "So, where is this guy that stole my car?" David reached in his pockets fishing out a set of car keys, seeming to not want to answer. "He's locked up over in Barnet City Jail. I'm about to go over there and see if I can I identify him."

Lisa furrowed her brow, worried about her father facing this person. "Is mom with you?" He grimaced, affirming, "Yes, she's in the car. Here are your keys. I dare say I'm not going to ask you to leave them under your floor mat again."

Lisa half smiled at his comment. He continued, beginning to smile himself, "Since all this happened, I wasn't able to get your tires changed out. I'll try to get that done for you tomorrow." She held up her hand, signaling that it wasn't a big deal. "We'll worry about it tomorrow. I'm just happy you got my car back for me."

David nodded. "Since the car is still in my name, it saved them asking me a bunch of questions about it." Lisa sighed. "Thank goodness." He gave her a wink and patted her on the hand. "Just be careful going home tonight." "I will. Love you." He headed for the door and turned back toward her. "Love you too."

Lisa tried to digest all that her father had told her as she waited on the customer. She grinned slightly after the older gentleman exited. "I can't wait to tell Roger about this."

∞

Roger stood in the parking lot of Barnet City Jail and looked at the gold Chevy Spark that sat in the parking lot. "Now how the hell did you get my rental car over here?" Richard tried to hide a smile. "Son, you wouldn't believe me if I told you."

Roger scratched his head. "Also, how did you get the State Police to let me go? They don't even know who I am." Richard ran his hand through his long hair, pushing it behind one ear, "Let's just say that I have the power to smooth matters out when too many explanations are required. I will tell you this: that gift was handed down to me by my father long before you were born."

Roger shook his head in disbelief at the whole situation. Richard looked at him intently, "Don't concern yourself about it. Right now, the only thing that should be on your mind is getting to Lisa. Her dad managed to get her car back to her."

He opened the door and slid behind the wheel, his duffel bag still neatly in the passenger seat. Roger pulled the door closed and looked up at his rescuer. "You had wanted me to tell you if I intended to come back to Mystery Hill and stay the next six months. That is what I intend to do after I save Lisa tonight. It is too dangerous for me to be wandering around, and I'm tired of being paranoid about every little thing I do possibly causing a terrible situation on some future event." Richard nodded. "I thought you might."

Roger started the car and spoke before pulling away. "I don't know how you did all of this but thank you. I'm sorry I have been so much trouble." Richard waved his hand at Roger in protest as he drove away. "You don't have to thank me."

Roger watched as Richard turned into a small spot in his mirror and disappeared from view. His attention turned to the road in front of him. A determination developed inside himself he'd never felt before. This was his last chance to save Lisa. If he didn't get to her before the accident, the happenings of the last two days would have been for nothing.

Roger pointed the car east, toward the river and headed to Monroe. "God, please be with me now. I can't live without Lisa! You know that she is my total existence. Please don't have me suffer through losing her again."

∞

Richard watched the little gold Chevy fade into the distance. All of

Roger's past and future possibilities which coursed through his head were starting to quiet, as all the possible paths began to merge together. In Richard's mind, time was not linear. Every outcome of Roger's life could be seen; every triumph and every failure. The young man's final outcome was still his own choice. As Roger had traveled back in time, Richard had simply given him a glimpse of other available paths.

A shadowy shape glided in the air and landed on its usual resting place on Richard's shoulder. He stroked the bird and turned to look into his infinite black orbs. "We'll not see him for a while, will we, Percy?"

Chapter Fourteen

Lisa busily buzzed about the store as she prepared to lock up. Even before the news of her car being stolen, it had been a challenging day on her nerves. She locked up the store and checked off her usual duties before arming the alarm. The employee door of the drug store closed with a slight click behind her as she approached her car.

The strong chill of the September wind burned her eyes as she inspected her recently returned ride. Everything on the outside looked as it always had. She opened the door and inspected the interior. The items in her glove compartment and console all seemed to be in their usual place. Nothing was missing.

Starting up the motor, she considered why someone would steal a car but not take any of its contents. She deduced that her would-be thief had other motives than simple petty theft.

Lisa looked into her mirror as she backed out of the parking lot. She could see small circles under her green eyes, proving it had been a long day.

Her mood lightened a bit at the thought of calling Roger when she got home. She knew he would crack a joke or tell some outlandish story to cheer her up. He always did and she loved him for it.

Turning onto the main highway and speeding up, she could feel a slight shimmy coming from the front part of her car. "Looks like Roger was right, I do need new tires," she thought as she turned on the radio.

One of her favorite songs whispered from the speakers, causing her to turn up the volume and begin to sing:

I feel revived again,
I am alive again.
You got me lifted and
Lifted you lift me up.

I feel revived again,
I'm energized again.
You got me lifted and
Lifted you lift me up.

A smile began to form on her face as she sang. The lyrics always reminded her of Roger because he truly lifted her up every single day. Lisa continued singing as she drummed the beat on her steering wheel. Her vehicle began to vibrate harder, causing her to slow down just a tad. "Come on now," she warned her car, "just get me home and we will get you fixed tomorrow."

Slowing down seemed to cause the shimmying to ease up, but she focused her senses as she made her way toward her apartment. As the song came to an end, Lisa entered the curve approaching her apartment complex. She could see a car headed in her direction.

As a precaution, she tapped her brakes slightly, hoping it would help with the vibration on the left side of her car. Lisa felt the left side of her car jump slightly as the steering wheel ripped from her grasp. She tried to grab the wheel just in time to see the glow of headlights from the oncoming car fill her windshield.

Lisa heard the sound of metal on metal and glass shattering all around as her body became weightless for just moment, followed by an abrupt jolt. Pain like a thousand blades shot all through her body as her senses quickly dulled and her vision went from white, to gray, to dark.

∞

Roger white knuckled the steering wheel of his rental car as he accelerated across the bridge leading into New Hampshire. It took everything within him not to exceed the speed limit as he reached the other end of the bridge. Having one run-in with the law was enough. He wasn't about to push his luck again.

He saw the sign for the Monroe city limits and made the appropriate turn toward Lisa's apartment. His body quivered with an uncontrollable panic as the fear that he may be too late soaked deep into his brain. A few stray tears coursed their way down his dirt smeared face.

A car driving about twenty miles under the speed limit slowed his trip. Roger mumbled curses under his breath, wishing the person in front of him would get off the road. Every time he would make an attempt to pass the car, another one from the opposite direction would block his way.

On the fifth instance of swerving into the left lane he finally succeeded in rocketing by the turtle paced car, the elderly driver giving Roger an angered glare as he passed.

Roger doubled his speed as he reached the rear entrance of Lisa's apartment complex. He sped through the parking lot to make sure she wasn't there, scanning every vehicle as he passed.

She wasn't there.

He dashed out the lot's exit and headed toward town. He kept cycling through his head how he would explain all of this to Lisa and her not think him a crazed lunatic.

Roger started the curve toward town and saw a familiar pair of headlights approaching in the left lane.

His heart raced with excitement. It had to be Lisa. He'd seen her car so many times before, the shape of the headlights glow was unmistakable. He started slowing, hoping to draw her attention as he passed by her car.

Roger saw dust, gravel, and pieces of shredded rubber erupt from her left, front wheel. He slammed his foot onto the brake, causing his vehicle to spin sideways in his lane.

As he spun, he could see Lisa's car veer into the left quarter panel of his car. Roger inhaled to scream as a yellowish-orange light flashed in his vision.

He could smell the undeniable odor of gasoline as the air in his lungs vanished. There was another enormous blaze of light, the smell of burning hair, and then all was dark.

Epilogue

Saturday, March 22, 2014

Over six months had passed since Roger had disappeared atop Mystery Hill. Gene stood in Barnet Cemetery with the girl whose heart he had finally managed to capture at his side. He looked into Heather's emerald pools and passed his hand down the length of her red hair before settling his palm next to hers.

Gene led her to the grave of Lisa Barnet and motioned toward her headstone. "This was Roger's fiancé, Lisa." Heather squeezed Gene's hand tightly. "This is the fiancé of your friend Roger, the guy who went missing?" He nodded slowly in response.

Heather studied the engraving on the headstone and then looked at Gene.

"The police have no idea what happened to him?" "Not a clue," he offered.

Gene knew where Roger had gone. He'd gone to save Lisa from the very fate that lay in front of where they both stood. The Spring Equinox had come and gone with no sign of Roger. Gene knew, deep down, that Roger was either trapped in the past or dead.

An icy chill crossed the cemetery and Gene heard footsteps behind him. He turned and almost dislocated Heather's arm trying to get her to run. A time-weathered figure threw his hands up as a calming gesture. "Gene! It's okay. I'm here to talk to you about Roger."

Richard approached them with a ring of smoke wafting around him from his pipe. Gene steadied himself and patted Heather's arm gently. "Wait right here."

He plodded up to the old man, noting Percy sitting on his shoulder, ever watchful. "What are you doing here, Richard?" Gene hissed from clenched teeth. "I'm here to tell you that your friend got his wish."

Gene shook his head and pointed squarely at Lisa's grave. "How is that exactly? Lisa's still here, dead and buried. He didn't save her and now he is missing." Richard motioned Gene to follow him.

Gene turned toward Heather. "Sweetie, will you wait for me by the car? Richard, his pet bird, and I need to have a little chat." She flashed him a reluctant look but complied.

Richard led him to the far edge of the cemetery to a grave directly in line with Lisa's. The grave was marked with a small footstone, the letters R.E.G. engraved into it.

Gene balled up his fists, refusing to admit to himself what he saw. "What the hell is this? Those are Roger's initials!"

Richard solemnly replied, "Time travel isn't a lucrative business, but I did what I could for him."

Gene lunged at the old man, but Percy dove toward his face, making him step back. "You son of a bitch! This is your fault!" His voice sounded shaky and fragmented.

The crow returned to his place on Richard's shoulder and scowled at Gene. Richard sighed. "No son, it isn't. I helped your friend obtain what he wanted." Gene straightened his backbone, trying to hide his fear and anger. "What he wanted? Death was not his wish! Do you think that is what he wanted?"

Richard lifted his wizened face to peer deep into Gene's eyes. "No. He loved Lisa more than anything in the world and could not live without her." Gene huffed, deflating slightly. Yes, I know! He said that constantly!"

"Son, Lisa was going to die. In her case, there was no way to prevent it. I gave him his wish, his wish to be with her forever." Gene backed a few steps away from Richard as the old man's words sank in. Richard continued, "I did not kill your friend. He would have died a miserable human being without Lisa, you know that. I gave him the opportunity to be with her when she left this world. Now they will be together for all eternity." Gene lowered his head, fighting back his tears. "Are...are you sure?"

Richard stepped forward and placed his hand on the younger man's shoulder. "Believe me when I tell you, he is truly happy." Gene looked in the direction of Heather, her beautiful frame resting on the fender of his car.

Gene's love for Heather paralleled what he knew Roger had felt for Lisa. He turned back and met Richard's eyes, finally seeing the truth in his words. Richard smiled at Gene; his pipe pushed to one side.

Percy twisted his head to and fro as a token of reassurance to Gene that, in another place, Roger and Lisa blissfully existed together forever.

Acknowledgments

To start out this acknowledgement, I want to thank Kristina Eaton for her support early in the production of *The Mystery Hill Series* by being the first book's beta-reader. She took on an extremely important role in editing this work's first draft many years ago, as well as her help with other works that I have co-authored.

Also, thanks to all the people that purchased any or all of my previous works. Without your support, none of these books would be possible.

Another great appreciation goes out to Stephanie White for her incredible cover art. Percy has never looked better!

Additionally, sincere thanks to Melissa Haddock for her help with early revisions of this book. Her eye for detail and her ability to ask the question, 'But why?' helped push me to take another look at the written word.

Complete heart-felt gratitude also goes out to Kellie Fowler-Glover, a woman of great intellect and a tremendous understanding of the written word. Her appreciation and discernment for myself and my writing is why this volume exists in its current form. I truly thank you for all your help in fine tuning my little work of 'historical fiction' into something that readers will find appealing.

Another thanks is due to the editor of the second edition of *A Twist In Time*, Gal Leopold. Her work behind the scenes to update the phrasing and cadence of my original story was invaluable to this new edition. The story is still at its heart in its original form, just with a few changes in terminology.

Finally, I thank our Heavenly Father. If it were not for Him, I would not be able to continue to bring these books to others. Thank you Lord for all you have done and continue to do in my life!

Mystery Hill Series

Book #1 – A Twist In Time
Book #2 – Times Not Traveled
Book #3 – COMING FALL 2021

By E. G. Glover
(Available on Kindle and paperback from
Relative Term Press)

The Fear Series

By L R Barrett-Durham and E. G. Glover
(Available on Kindle and paperback from
Van Pelt Press)

"This first book in the 'Fear' Series will keep you on the edge of your seat."

"Very unpredictable, exciting, nail biting, and pretty steamy at times."

"From the first page it sucks you right in and you literally do not want to put it down!"

~Reviews from Amazon.com
Book #1 - Fear the Beast Within

"Excellent!.... Mind blowing!....."

"I absolutely LOVED the first book of the series, Fear the Beast Within, and didn't think it could get any better, but I was SO WRONG!!!!"

"Grady and Leia have done it again!"

"I only put the book down to go to work and when I came home I picked it right back up and didn't put it down till I was finished."

"They really knocked it out of the park with this one! I love getting to know each character!"

"I'm not afraid to admit that I've been in love with Geo Riner since Saxton Lyall first stepped into Mystics Book Emporium way back in Book #1. When I found out that the 3rd book was going to be Geo's story, I was beyond excited."

About the Author

(Photo by Anne Glover)

E. G. Glover currently lives in northwest Alabama. When diagnosed with multiple sclerosis in 2010, he took on writing as a full-time venture. Alongside his *Mystery Hill Series* of time travel fiction, he has also co-written several books based within the realm of paranormal romance, *The Fear Series*, with story collaborator, L R Barrett-Durham.

When not working as an author or attending duties as creator and founder of *WHoBoX Industries*, Glover enjoys time with his two daughters, his wife Kellie, and visits from her two children. In his spare time, he is a collector of *Retro-Electro*; known to most as antiqued home entertainment audio/video equipment. Glover also holds a deep love for television and cinema based in the science fiction realm, *Doctor Who* being his favorite piece of work in the sci-fi genre.

You can find E. G. Glover via social media at:
http://www.facebook.com/EGGlover1976

or

http://www.twitter.com/RelativeTerm